"Open for m
mouth hot

Restlessly, Shea shifted her legs and arched her body, granting his request. And she was oh, so sweetly rewarded. Slowly, delicately, he stroked her tender flesh until she clutched his shoulder. "Reese?"

"Just let it happen, darlin'."

And she did. Twice. Each time her body tensed, the heat building to an unbearable level, then a shuddering release that was no release at all because it stoked the hunger. Finally his clever fingers drove her up, almost to the peak, but not over. "Please. Oh, Reese, please."

He slid his hands beneath her hips to bring her to him, and she met him halfway. And then he slowly, completely filled her. She tensed for a half second, then with a deep moan she began to move against him, rotating her hips in the ageless dance to a wild rhythm. Harder, faster, until the wildness swept them both up and over into a shattering climax.

When his breathing slowed, Reese looked down at Shea and smiled. "Better than good?"

"Much. Wonderful. Delicious." She blushed. "I didn't expect…that is, I never—"

"Well, you have now," he teased. "And I gotta say…you, lady, are one fast learner."

Dear Reader,

I had such a great time participating in Temptation's first MAIL ORDER MEN series, the opportunity to do it again proved to be irresistible. Throw in a gorgeous, lonely cowboy looking for love, a baby, secret pen pals and lots of fun—who could resist?

And speaking of irresistible, my hero Reese Barrett definitely *is.* After creating him as the hero's best friend in *After the Loving,* I just couldn't forget him. So, of course, I had to tell his story. Calm and steady as the stars, Reese thinks he knows exactly what kind of life he wants and what type of woman he needs. Until Shea Alexander shows up. She turns his life upside down then right side up in a way he never expected. So join me for another trip to Sweetwater Springs, Texas, where tall, dark and wickedly handsome Reese meets the woman of his dreams *and* his fantasies.

Sincerely,

Sandy Steen

Sandy Steen
THE LONE WOLF

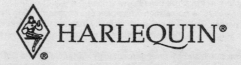

TORONTO • NEW YORK • LONDON
AMSTERDAM • PARIS • SYDNEY • HAMBURG
STOCKHOLM • ATHENS • TOKYO • MILAN • MADRID
PRAGUE • WARSAW • BUDAPEST • AUCKLAND

To Brenda Chin—
Patient, perceptive, editor extraordinaire

ISBN 0-373-25791-0

THE LONE WOLF

Copyright © 1998 by Sandy Steen.

1

IF IT WASN'T FOR THE FACT that the man was his best friend and one helluva nice guy, Reese would have liked nothing better than to punch Cade McBride right in the nose. And for no other reason than the fact that he had everything Reese wanted: a beautiful, adoring wife, a baby on the way and a Texas-size slice of pure happiness.

Of course it wasn't Cade's fault that he was lonely and aching for a woman, Reese reminded himself. The fault, if there was any, lay in his own inability to settle for anything less than the woman of his dreams. A woman like Cade's wife, Belle. A woman with courage and a gentle spirit, intelligence tempered with wisdom. In short, a perfect woman. But he was beginning to think his friend had snagged the last one.

The couple in question were standing a few yards away, kissing each other goodbye as if they'd be apart for days instead of the hour or so it took for Belle's weekly appointment with her obstetrician. With one booted foot resting on the foot-high rock ledge surrounding the shrubbery in front of the office of the Farentino Ranch and winery, Reese watched the scene, as hungry as a half-starved wolf at the end of a long, lean winter. As much as he hated to admit it, the plain, unavoidable truth was that he envied the hell out of Cade McBride.

Finally, thankfully, Belle climbed into her shiny new red Suburban and drove away. Cade turned and headed for the office wearing the damn silliest grin Reese had ever seen. God, he was jealous.

Cade stopped short at the look on his friend's face. "What's with you?"

"Nothing."

"Yeah? That frown you're wearing's got furrows deep enough to plant. Problem at the winery?"

"Nope."

Now Cade frowned. "Anything going on around here I should know about?"

Reese shook his head.

"Isn't today your day off?"

"Yeah."

"Then what the hell are you doing hanging around the office?"

"Thought I'd see if you needed a hand. I used to do this for a living, remember?"

"Oh, I remember. I'm just having a hard time figuring out why you'd come looking for work when you don't have to."

Reese shrugged. "Might as well be busy."

"Just killin' time, huh?"

"Yeah."

"Then you're either crazy, bored or horny. And since I've known you most of your life, and spent way too many years rodeoing with you, I can testify that you're as sane as the next guy. And the word *boredom* isn't even in your vocabulary. That only leaves—"

"Back off."

Cade shoved his hat back on his head and grinned. "Hit a nerve, did I?"

"Listen, Ace—"

"Seems to me we've had this conversation before and I still say you're just too picky."

"Selective."

"It amounts to the same thing if you're sittin' home alone on a Saturday night, but—"

"I'm lookin' for more than a one-night stand. And if I remember correctly, you were pretty damned picky yourself. How many years had you been pining after Belle before she asked you to marry her?"

"Three, but we're not talking about me, and you do have a flaw or two, you know."

"Such as?"

"Reese, you're my best friend and have been since grade school, but to be honest, you're a dinosaur."

"What the hell does that mean?"

"You're a throwback to the fifties. You still think the woman should stay home and take care of the kids."

"And what's wrong with making raising kids a career? It's probably the hardest job in the world."

"I agree, but women today want to make that choice for themselves, not have it made for them. And most of them would like to have a family *and* a career, if possible. Your problem is you've spent too much time with buckle bunnies."

"You ought to know. You were standing right next to me most of the time."

"Yeah, well, those days are long gone, and I don't miss 'em."

"So, that's it? That's my major hang-up?"

Cade cleared his throat. "That, and maybe one other."

Reese folded his arms across his chest. "Go on."

"Well, for the most part you're a go-along-and-get-along kinda guy, but..." Cade shrugged. "Maybe it's your background. Lord knows, you've been involved in enough brawls over your Cherokee heritage over the years. But still, you don't budge worth a damn."

"Like you do?"

"No. You and I are too much alike on that. In fact, my temper is probably quicker to spark than yours. But you're kinda standoffish, a loner, and just about the most stubborn guy I ever knew. And sometimes I think you carry that great stone-faced attitude too far. A trait that will not stand you in good stead with a woman. All those years with no one to consider but myself didn't help when it came time to adjust to living with Belle." Cade grinned. "Of course, I gotta say it's sure worth the effort."

"Great, you've got what you want, so now you're the expert on finding a good woman?"

"All I'm saying is you got to give a little to get a little if you're really interested in having a relationship. And it doesn't take an expert to know you'll never find a good woman if you don't go looking."

"I've looked."

"You telling me that there's not one female in

the whole of Sweetwater Springs, Texas, that interests you?"

Reese gave Cade a hard look. "It's a small town."

"What about Lubbock? It's all of seven miles away, or are you opposed to an out-of-town girl?"

"You're a riot, McBride."

"'Cause if it's an import you're interested in, Belle's friend should arrive from Austin in a couple of months."

"The business genius, Alexandra something-or-other?"

"Shea Alexander. I've only seen a picture from when she and Belle were in college, but she's got a great—"

"Personality. Where have I heard that before? No thanks. I'll find my own woman."

"Body."

"What?"

"She's got a terrific body. Even Belle says so. And you know when a woman pays another woman a compliment like that…"

Reese sighed. "I just told you I'm lookin' for more. You know, you make a much better foreman than you do a Dear Abby. If I wanted your advice—"

"Okay, okay." Cade held up his hands in surrender. "I know when I've drawn a mean bronc. Let's check the work schedule and see if we can't find you some real *physical* labor."

Once they were inside the office, Cade leaned across the desk of Dorothy Fielding, secretary for the Farentino ranch, snagged the clipboard holding a copy of a two-week work schedule and scanned the printout. "Got some fence down to the northwest, and—" he flipped the page "—we're building four new stalls. How 'bout it? Wanna take out your frustrations on some helpless two-by-fours?"

"Sounds perfect."

"You got it. Matter of fact, I'll change into some workin' clothes and join you." In the process of replacing the clipboard Cade stopped, then picked up the magazine sitting on the desk. "Hey now. This looks like the solution to your problem."

"What?"

He handed Reese the magazine, *Texas Men*. "I love to tease Dorothy about these things, accusin' her of droolin' over beefcake on her lunch hour. She buys 'em all the time."

"What are you talking about?"

"This." He thumped the magazine. "It's a hunk catalog. Guys send in a picture and their vital statistics. Women browse through, pick out a guy they think looks interesting and write him."

Reese took the magazine, thumbing through the pages. "Advertising for a girlfriend?"

"Or a wife."

Reese handed the magazine back to his friend. "Get serious."

"I'm dead serious. And if you're too shy or just too dog-faced ugly to send a picture, they've got a personals section in the back. Sort of a blind date by mail."

"And just how do you know so much about this particular publication?"

"I told you. Dorothy's always got a copy lying

around. She won't admit it, but I'll bet she sub-scribes."

"I couldn't ever do anything like that. Might as well just hang a sign around my neck with my phone number on it and parade down Main Street."

Cade tossed the magazine onto Dorothy's desk. "You're a hard man to satisfy." With a quick, wicked grin, he put a healthy distance between them before he added, "Come to think of it, that's probably how you got in this fix in the first place."

"Why, you sorry son of a—"

"Is that any way to talk to your best friend?" Cade raced for the door. A rubber-band missile hit the crown of his hat and ricocheted off just as he made a strategic retreat.

Grinning, Reese was right on his heels. "You'll pay for that," he called out before heading to the barn for his prescribed manual labor.

He'd put the idea of advertising for a woman completely out of his mind until he and Cade came out of the barn later that afternoon, hot, tired and in need of a shower. Heading for his cabin while his friend made his way up to the main house, Reese glanced over his shoulder in time to see Belle walk out to greet her husband. Heedless of grime and sweat, she wrapped her arms around him, got as close as her nicely rounded tummy would permit and gave him a kiss that had Reese's heart beating faster just watching. Maybe he *was* asking for too much. Because that's what he wanted—a woman who would kiss him like that, clean or dirty, rain or shine, for the rest of his life.

He yanked off his hat, wiped the sweat from his

face with the back of his forearm and glanced at the office. He'd come up with at least a dozen reasons he should forget about the magazine lying on the secretary's desk. If he stood there long enough, he could probably come up with a dozen more.

"Aw, hell," he mumbled, walking toward the office.

Back in his cabin fifteen minutes later, he opened a beer, sat down on the sofa, propped his dusty boots on the coffee table and started to read.

It didn't take him long to realize *Texas Men* was no cheesy, fly-by-night setup. The publishers had done a first-rate job, not only with the way they handled the interviews and photos, but with the well-thought-out security plan to ensure no weirdos could get names and addresses without permission. All correspondence was sent to the magazine then forwarded, unopened, until the writers of the letters made the decision to give out their actual addresses. The magazine offered tips on how to begin correspondence, deal with unwanted mail, even how to handle kinky or downright pornographic letters. Of course, Reese only intended to do the personals ad, and since he was easily identified with the winery and wanted to avoid trading on the Farentino name, he wouldn't use his own name.

Intended?

Until that moment he hadn't realized he'd already made up his mind to contact the magazine. And as for choosing the personals, well…they didn't require a photo—a photo that would clearly show his Indian heritage.

Not that he wasn't proud of his Cherokee blood.

He was. But he was the first to admit it had caused some problems over the years. Granted, he was younger then, more likely to look for trouble. Unfortunately, not everyone was free of prejudice.

Not even his own mother.

She'd thought loving a Cherokee man would be wildly exciting. It was the most daring thing she'd ever done and certainly came as a shock to her wealthy Baltimore family. But she had never stopped to think about what it would be like to have a half-breed son. After four years of struggling against a prejudice she hadn't even known she harbored, she left. No shouting, no tears. One afternoon she simply took Reese to a neighbor's house, kissed him goodbye and drove away. That pain had stayed with him a long time. Only since meeting Caesar Farentino and discovering a love of winemaking had he been able to make peace with his past. The only residue was his inability to completely trust a woman.

The mental tug-of-war over whether he was withholding his name and photo to protect himself or the winery didn't last long. He was comfortable with who and what he was, and personally, he couldn't care less what people thought of him. Cade, Belle and the reputation of the winery were another matter altogether.

He reached over to the table at one end of the sofa and grabbed a pencil and a pad of paper. So, he would omit a couple of facts. Otherwise, he would stay as close to the truth as possible, saying he lived and worked on a ranch, had done some rodeoing in the past and basically wanted to settle down with a good woman.

Poised to write, Reese stared at the blank piece of paper. He'd never done anything like this in his life and he didn't mind admitting it was a little scary. What if he got letters from a bunch of lovesick old maids? Or married women looking for a thrill?

Or worse. What if he received no letters at all?

"This is crazy. You should have your head examined, Barrett," he told himself, even as he scanned the information, found the deadline for submission and realized if he mailed his letter tomorrow morning he would just make it. Maybe it *was* crazy, but he was tired of being a lone wolf.

He wanted a mate.

Reese downed half of his beer then stared at the magazine. Hell, why not? What did he have to lose? It was only a letter. How much trouble could he get into just writing a letter?

But even as he asked himself that question, he knew he was serious about finding a woman he could share his life with. And it didn't make a whole lot of difference how he found her. Reese started to write.

Serious, the headline stated.

Austin, Texas, three weeks later

SHEA ALEXANDER WOULD rather have a root canal than sit idle for more than ten minutes, which was ironic, because she had been waiting more than half an hour to get in to see her dentist. It was only a routine visit, but obviously his staff had double booked him because she wasn't alone. There were… She glanced around, realizing the other waiting patients were all female. Six of them. Shea couldn't remember ever seeing the small outer office this crowded. Dr. Harrington's practice was definitely booming.

Bored, she reached for a nearby magazine, changed her mind when she noticed the title, then did a double take. There was her dentist, smiling back at her from the cover of *Texas Men*.

Good Lord, the man was bare-chested and wearing a cowboy hat!

Strictly out of curiosity, she flipped through the pages until she found the article on David Harrington, D.D.S., along with another photo much like the one on the cover. After reading his "vital statistics," not to mention comments about his thriving practice, Shea suddenly understood why his waiting room was brimming with female patients. She looked at the other women. They ranged in age from early twenties to early thirties and were all dressed to kill, or at least dressed to show off whatever they considered their best asset. The one with great legs wore a tight, short skirt. Not bad, Shea admitted. One with a drop-dead gorgeous face had flawless makeup and red hair thick and lustrous enough to look as if she had just modeled for a shampoo commercial. Another had an absolutely eye-catching bustline, and store-bought or not, it was hard to ignore.

A bunch of peahens waiting for the peacock.

Ridiculous. They were so obvious it was embarrassing. Shea was suddenly disgusted with her own sex. And, she thought, glancing at her watch, she was going to be late for an extremely impor-

tant meeting. There was nothing to do but re-
schedule her appointment. As she rose and
walked to the reception desk, the woman with the
impossible-to-ignore chest stepped up beside her
and inquired how much longer it would be before
the dentist could see her.

Shea hated the fact that so often women were
judged by the size of their cleavage rather than
their brains, and she had always done her part to
fight such prejudice. As an intellectual, she re-
jected the traditional fashion and figure competition between females. As a woman, she instinctively tugged at the hem of her fitted jacket,
emphasizing her own natural, and if she did say
so herself, generous endowments.

"Excuse me," Shea said to the receptionist.
When she didn't receive an immediate response,
she absently rolled the magazine into a tube, tapping one end against her palm. "Excuse me," she
repeated in a voice that had commanded more
than one CEO's attention. "Please tell Dr. Harrington that I had a meeting and I'll call to resched-
ule."

Shea didn't even realize she still had the copy of
Texas Men until she was almost to her car. She
started to return it, then decided there wasn't
enough time. Never one to carelessly leave papers
loose in her car, she popped the double latches on
her leather briefcase and slipped the magazine
neatly inside before dashing to her meeting. A
meeting that ran far longer than she had anticipated.

By the time Shea stepped inside her condo near
Austin's Lake Travis four hours later, she was

dead tired and her feet hurt. She pitched her briefcase onto the sofa and collapsed beside it. She had
just kicked her shoes off when the phone rang.

"Oh, no," she moaned. "Whoever you are, go
away." After four persistent rings, she gave up
and answered. "If you're selling something, forget
it."

"Shea?"

"Belle." Shea smiled, the voice of her best friend
banishing some of her fatigue. "How are you?"

"Fat. I've got at least six weeks to go and I'm already big as a house."

"I doubt that."

"No kidding. I can barely get out of a chair
without help."

"Which I'm sure Cade is more than happy to
supply."

There was a long, rather contented-sounding
sigh, and Shea knew her friend was smiling.

"He's been wonderful. But you'll see for yourself soon enough. That's why I called. Just wanted
to make sure nothing had come up that might interfere with you pinch-hitting for me."

"No, and nothing will. I've got a new project in
the works, but it won't be up and running for at
least three months, so our plan is still solid."

"You're a lifesaver."

Shea could have said the same of her best and
only real friend. Her friendship with Belle Farentino McBride had given her the only normal relationship in her life. "I'm just happy I can do this
for you, particularly since I missed your wedding.
Make that weddings."

"The first one was so rushed, and the second,

well, it wasn't your fault your flight from Hong Kong got grounded in London because of fog."

"I know, but what kind of a person misses her best friend's wedding?"

"Don't be silly. When you get here, we can watch the video together and cry at all the appropriate parts." After a pause, Belle asked, "Are you okay?"

"Sure. Why do you ask?"

"I don't know, you just sound...down."

"Not really. Just tired." It was a lie, but Shea didn't feel up to talking about the restlessness she'd experienced the last few months, despite a horrendous work schedule. It was nothing serious, just nagging doubts and a general malaise, but for tonight she didn't want to think about it, much less talk about it. "So tell me, have you bought out all the baby stores within a fifty-mile radius?"

Belle laughed. "I didn't have to. Cade can't pass any kind of store without buying something. And since we decided to do this the old-fashioned way and be surprised at the sex, this baby already has a Dallas Cowboys football helmet and a Barbie doll."

"Covering all his bases, huh?"

"He's out of control. I've threatened to take his checkbook away from him, but every time I do, he shows up wearing a silly grin and holding some outrageously cute stuffed animal."

"Let's pray he's still that eager after the first three o'clock feeding."

"Are you kidding me? He's devoured every child care book he can get his hands on, reading about breast versus bottle feeding and on and on. If he's this obsessive now, no telling what he'll be like once the baby's here.''

All of which sounded like blissful normalcy to Shea. She wondered if Belle knew how lucky she was. "I'm sure things will settle down after the baby arrives. Listen to me talking as if I have a clue about these things. I don't think I've actually held a baby more than a couple of times in my life.''

"You'll take to it when it's your turn.''

"If I ever get a turn,'' Shea mumbled.

"What?''

"I'm sure I'll learn. Listen, I hate to cut this short, but I've got a stack of reports to wade through before tomorrow.''

"All right. Take care of yourself and I'll see you in a few weeks.''

"You, too.''

Shea hung up the phone and stared at it for several seconds. Now she had a name for her restlessness.

Loneliness.

Listening to Belle talk about her husband and the baby she was carrying crystallized the image of loneliness into a focus so sharp it was painful. And there was envy. She loved Belle like the sister she'd never had, and wished her nothing but happiness always, but...

She envied that happiness. A loving husband. A baby on the way.

Would her turn ever come?

"In order to get pregnant one must be exposed. And from where you're standing, old girl, prospects of stumbling across the love of your life are getting slimmer by the second."

If not because of age, then attitude. She wasn't exactly a goody-goody or a nun, although she could qualify on the celibacy even though she did date occasionally.

Occasionally?

Shea sighed. "Now, there's a euphemism for 'in your dreams' if ever I heard one."

She did have a vague memory of going to a must-attend formal company function with a handsome vice president of marketing several months back, but the event and the man had been lackluster to say the least. If she was honest with herself, she couldn't entirely blame her escort for the less-than-memorable date. The fact was, Shea was much more comfortable with profit and loss statements than affairs of the heart. She desperately wanted a relationship. She just hadn't a clue how to get, much less maintain, one.

The only child of highly intelligent parents, she still saw herself as the quintessential nerd when it came to the opposite sex. Her experience in that area was limited to one brief and unimpressive night with a co-worker she met on her first job out of college. He was a fellow nerd and they developed a friendship. Her mistake was in thinking there was a possibility for anything more. She could honestly say that if what she had experienced was all there was to sex, she'd pass. There certainly hadn't been any fireworks or bells ringing. All she could remember was feeling confused and inadequate. Technically, she wasn't a virgin. Practically speaking, she was a babe in the woods.

Too bad there wasn't a school she could attend to learn the finer points of flirting and how to attract men. With postgraduate studies in making love and making relationships work. Actually, she attracted men easily enough, but it wasn't due to her dazzling smile or sparkling wit. She had a great body. Pure and simple. She hadn't planned it that way or spent time in a gym to achieve it. Her lush curves were strictly a matter of genes. But she didn't want a man that was only interested in her body. The man she wanted would have to appreciate her intellect and her spirit and...

"Who are you kidding? You're smart enough to see the truth when it's right in front of you."

And when Shea looked into the mirror, she didn't see a beauty. She saw good bone structure, healthy skin, clear eyes and manageable hair. For all of her wishes for an ordinary life, she'd never included her looks. On that score, she'd been ordinary since the day she was born. Not that she considered herself homely. But she didn't have to be told her looks weren't the kind that inspired men to poetry or proposals. A critical self-assessment produced four pluses and minuses. On the plus side she had brains and drive. On the minus, she had nothing-special looks, zero self-confidence where men were concerned and a tender heart.

"Okay, that's three on the minus side, but who's counting." Maybe she should add "talks to herself."

The tender heart was a well-kept secret even from her parents. Her intellect was the cover-up, and it had worked well. She had learned how to survive and succeed in the male-dominated world of business and high finance not only because of her talent and drive, but also because she kept her vulnerability hidden. She had been thought of as a nerd for far too long to risk letting someone close enough to see her vulnerability. Fighting off depression, Shea reached for her briefcase and opened it.

"You've never let a man get close enough to appreciate your brilliant mind because you're a total dud at holding a simple conversation that isn't about market trends, portfolios and returns on investments."

All right, so she used her job as a defense against appearing totally inept when it came to dealing with men. Admitting it didn't make it any easier to change.

"I need a curriculum on kissing and a seminar on sex, followed by an advanced course on—"

She pulled a report out of her briefcase and out came the copy of *Texas Men* she had accidentally taken from the dentist's office. Spurred on by an urge she preferred to label curiosity rather than voyeurism, she set the report aside and opened the magazine. At least she could fantasize. And fantasize she did. Until finally, mere daydreams left a bitter taste in her mouth and an emptiness in her heart.

"Men. A whole book full of them and what good does it do me?"

Page after page of men. Hunks, almost all of them. Even the ones that weren't model gorgeous had at least one or two qualities that made them attractive. All those fantastic bodies, bedroom eyes and sexy smiles. And none of it for her.

"A lot of women with more guts than me—" she flipped to the first page, which outlined the steps for corresponding "—are going to follow a few simple rules and regulations and end up with a husband or, at the very least, some hot sex."

And *simple* was the right word to describe the procedure for writing to the featured men. The entire system was well thought out to ensure those wanting to remain anonymous could be so. Perhaps it was the anonymity that sparked the idea. Perhaps it was just plain old-fashioned loneliness. Whatever the reason, Shea suddenly realized she might just have stumbled across the perfect way to educate herself in Seduction 101.

Correspondence school.

"No, an experiment. Controlled, long-distance and low risk."

What could be simpler? And why hadn't she thought of something like this before? An experiment to test and possibly enhance her inadequate skills with men without having to experience the agony of awkward silences and trying to make small talk. A brilliant idea if she did say so herself.

But how exactly did one go about conducting such an experiment? she wondered, scanning page after page of smiling males ranging in age from early twenties to late fifties. What qualifiers could she use? Now, totally intrigued with the idea, Shea grabbed her laptop computer and began making notes on what she was looking for in a man.

Age? "Mid-thirties sounds about right."

Occupation? "Optional."

Athletic? "Not a sports nut, but enough to keep trim."

Hobbies and interests? "Anything but finance."

Background? "A large family would be nice. God, I hated being an only child."

Education? "Preferably college, but not mandatory."

Strange, but until this moment she'd never given much thought to the kind of man she wanted. Now, surveying her notes, she realized the profile wasn't as precise as she would have thought. Maybe because she had so little experience with men.

"A situation I am about to remedy," she said to the glossy color photo of a lawyer from Houston who wanted to befriend a woman with a passion for skiing. "Sorry, Counselor." She moved on to the next unwitting participant in her experiment, then the next.

She decided on four as a good number for her test, selecting what she considered to be a cross section of men from the front section of the magazine. Then she flipped to the personals section. After several pages of what she felt amounted to a lot of guys looking for love in all the wrong places, she came across an interesting ad.

Serious, the headline read.

I'm thirty-four, honest, reasonably ambitious and with only a few bad habits. I live on a ranch in the Panhandle and enjoy outdoor work. I'm looking for a woman with courage and a gentle spirit, intelligence tempered with wisdom. A woman interested in family values and simple pleasures like watching the sun set on the caprock.

Maybe the fact that he had been so up-front about "only a few bad habits" appealed to her. Or maybe it was the mention of the sunset that snagged her attention. Whatever the reason, he sounded like a nice, normal guy. He probably only had a high school education, but that was fine with her. The last thing she needed was someone with the same nerdy intelligence she had. Shea decided to expand her test number to five, adding Mr. Serious, aka number 2138, to her list. Now that she had her experimental, albeit unknowing, test subjects, it was time to compose her letter.

Never at a loss when it came to writing detailed financial reports, Shea discovered writing about herself was not only uncomfortable but boring. That was the very reason, she reminded herself, that she had decided to conduct this experiment in the first place. Besides, to be honest, she wasn't happy being Shea Alexander, lady financial whiz.

So, who did she want to be?

Without hesitation she fell back on a fantasy she had cherished since adolescence. A wish list that included being a beautiful high school cheerleader, a good, but not dazzling, college student majoring in primary education, followed by a job as a kindergarten teacher.

An ordinary existence, but one Shea would trade her current life for in a heartbeat. Particularly if the right man went with it. As she finished composing her letter, she debated about whether or not to use her real name.

Shea smiled. "Why not go for the whole enchilada?" she said, signing the name she had always wished she had. Natalie. She printed out five letters for the various men, using their assigned numbered addresses, sealed them in individual envelopes, then put them in a manila envelope addressed to the magazine. Fearing she might lose her nerve, Shea put more than an adequate number of stamps on the envelope, picked up her purse and keys and walked across the lush garden of the gated community of condos to the mailbox near the office. Quickly, she shoved the envelope into the slot then took a step back.

For better or worse, there was no going back.

2

"WELL, LOOKIE YONDER," Alvin Delworthy said, pointing toward the post office.

"Where?" Toothless Smitty Lewis half rose from one of the benches he, Alvin and Old Walt had all but homesteaded on the Sweetwater Springs town square. "Where you pointin'?"

"Right there. Comin' outta the post office."

Old Walt glanced up, then went back to his whittling. "You're gettin' plumb senile, Alvin. Any fool knows that's Reese Barrett."

"Well." Alvin hooked his thumbs in his pockets and rocked back on his boot heels. "Just wonder what he's got in that envelope tucked under his arm."

Smitty studied the tall winery manager walking along the other side of the street, then looked at his companions. "I reckon it's mail, don't you?"

Old Walt stopped whittling long enough to roll his eyes, then looked at Alvin. "You been hangin' 'round Pearl Dorsey an awful lot lately. And since she's the postmaster—"

"Mistress. Postmistress. You got to stay up with the times, Walt."

Old Walt pointed a bony finger at his friend. "You know somethin' you ain't tellin', and that's a fact."

"Maybe. Maybe not." Alvin smirked.

Smitty's eyes gleamed. "Whatcha got? Somethin' spicy?"

"All I know is Reese come into town last month and rented himself his own post office box and he's been comin' once a week to pick up his—" Alvin paused for effect "—private mail."

"Whatcha reckon he's gettin' in a big envelope like that? Bet he's subscribin' to one of them girlie magazines."

"Don't rightly know, but it sure seems funny that he'd get himself a post office box after getting his mail at the winery all these years."

The three men exchanged glances, then nodded their mutual agreement.

Old Walt set aside the hunk of cherry laurel wood just beginning to take the shape of the coyote he was carving, stood up and headed across the street. The other two were right on his heels.

"Hey there, Reese," he called out.

Reese stopped, nodded to the three. Thankfully, he had been in the ranch office the day Dorothy's monthly issue of *Texas Men* had arrived and he had noted the distinctive return address label. He immediately contacted the magazine and asked that all correspondence from them be forwarded to him blind. It wouldn't do for the biggest gossips in town to know he had bought a copy of the magazine, much less been writing to women he'd never seen. "How you boys doin'?"

"We ain't complainin'."

Alvin glanced at the manila envelope beneath Reese's right arm. "Been to the post office, huh?"

"Yeah. Once you get on a mailing list for a catalog, they start coming by the dozen."

"I reckon." Old Walt turned his head to see if he could get a better look.

"Say, your boots is shinin' and looks like you got on a new shirt. You're all duded up. Where you off to this morning?" Smitty asked.

"Got to drive into Lubbock and pick up a friend of Belle's. She's going to help at the winery when Belle's baby comes."

"Gonna be pretty soon now, I guess," Old Walt said.

Smitty grinned. "Hot damn. Bet Cade's chompin' at the bit."

"That's putting it mildly. Well, wish I had time to visit, boys, but I gotta meet that plane. See ya." Without giving them a chance for more questions, Reese walked on, leaving the three staring after him.

Alvin looked at Old Walt. "You see who it was from?"

"Nope. Couldn't make out a name on the return address."

"What you reckon it is?" Smitty asked.

"Don't know." Old Walt rubbed his stubbled chin. "But we'll find out sooner or later, and that's a fact."

FORTY-FIVE MINUTES LATER Reese sat cooling his heels in the Lubbock airport. The plane was late and he was not thrilled. Truthfully, his irritation was the tip of an iceberg of uncertainty. He'd never met a genius before, much less a female genius. Cade had been right about spending time

with too many buckle bunnies. Not that he didn't
think he could hold his own with Ms. Supersmart
Alexander. His college degree might have taken
six years, including a lot of night and correspondence courses, but he'd graduated with honors.
No, his main concern was how he and the lady
whiz kid would get along. After all, they would
have to work together until Belle was ready to re-
sume running the winery. And even though the
highly respected Farentino label was distributed
in more than thirty states and six European coun-
tries, the company and its less than fifty employees functioned very much like an extended family.
Everyone knew everyone else, and the atmo-
sphere was relaxed and comfortable. For all her
generosity in offering to help out an old friend,
Shea Alexander might not mix. Only time would
tell.

Reese glanced at his watch. No telling how
much longer the plane might be delayed. He
picked up a discarded copy of the newspaper that
had been left on the seat beside him, but he didn't
really want to read about a bond election or im-
provements being made in Mackenzie State Park.
He wanted to reread the letter in his shirt pocket.

His fourth letter from Natalie.

He hadn't known what to expect when he com-
posed the ad for *Texas Men* magazine. When the
first batch of correspondence arrived, he'd been
overwhelmed at the response. Over forty letters.
Despite the number, it didn't take him long to
weed out the thrill seekers from the serious. Then
he read Natalie's letter and lost interest in the rest.

Two months ago he wouldn't have dreamed he

could feel the way he did about a women he'd never seen. But Natalie was a dream come true. Sweet, tenderhearted and with a delightfully sunny nature, she had captured his heart with her very first letter. So much so that he was considering giving her his real name and actual address. Given his usual wait-and-see policy where women were concerned, he couldn't explain the immediate sense of connection he'd felt. Or the feeling that she was exactly as she presented herself, refreshing and honest. He touched his shirt pocket, tempted to pull out the letter and read it for the third time, but changed his mind. The plane could arrive any minute. Besides, he preferred to be alone when he read Natalie's letters.

Just then the delayed flight's arrival was announced and he headed for gate three.

Standing just outside the gate so he could get a good look at the deplaning passengers, Reese waited. Belle had intended to give him a picture to help him identify her friend, but she hadn't felt well this morning and Cade couldn't find the photo. He'd had to settle for a description aided by his mental image of what he expected Shea Alexander to look like. She would probably be wearing a business suit and tasteful, expensive shoes with a "sensible" heel height. Her hair would be cut short or worn in a neat french twist, and of course she would be carrying a briefcase. There were two women that fit the description, but only one near Belle's age. When she stopped to talk to the ticket agent, he approached her, then stood several feet back, leaning his right shoulder against a post, and waited.

Oh yeah, this was undoubtedly the high-powered Ms. Alexander, he decided, listening to her register a detailed complaint about a flight attendant's response to a request. This woman was all business. He folded his arms across his chest and waited for the lady to finish.

Shea Alexander spotted Reese Barrett the minute she walked through gate three. He was hard to miss. Her first thought was that the snapshot Belle had sent didn't do him justice. He wasn't just good-looking, he was... The best word she could find to describe him was *breathtaking*. Fit didn't even begin to describe his body. And that face, Shea thought. His jaw and cheekbones looked as if they had been sculpted by a Native American artist. Strength and determination were stamped into that face.

Born and raised in Texas, she was no stranger to men in jeans, boots and Western shirts. They were part of the landscape, as common as houseflies. But there was nothing common about the way Reese Barrett's jeans fit his long, powerful legs, or the way the muscles in his arms strained against the cotton shirtsleeves. He was tall, at least six foot three. His hair was a little too long, almost curling over his collar, but it only added to his roguish appeal. She might not have had much experience with sex, but even she recognized sexy when she saw it. And judging from the way he was eyeing the curvy strawberry blonde in the tailored suit, he wasn't totally unaware of his masculine appeal. Leaning against a post, arms folded, he seemed to be leisurely enjoying the view, just waiting for the woman to notice him.

Tall, dark and handsome. Not pretty handsome, because his face looked as if it had some well-earned character. Rugged, but definitely in the good-looking category. Probably a ladies' man. Exactly the kind that always threw her for a loop, made her act and sound like the village idiot. Old insecurities she had thought subdued wiggled free of restraint and began crowding her mind. He was definitely nothing like the pen pal who had quickly become her favorite, Mr. Serious.

Shea smiled, her mounting tension momentarily eased. Mr. Serious, the most productive subject in her experiment. His letters were the highlight of her week. She had learned more from corresponding with him over the last few weeks than she had from her entire dating experience. He was the perfect subject, strong, honest, hardworking, and best of all, he just wanted an ordinary life with someone he treasured. He was so perfect, in fact, that she was beginning to feel uncomfortable with the fantasy she had created to entice him.

She looked at Reese Barrett. From where she was standing, he and Mr. Serious were probably polar opposites. The only thing the manager of the Farentino winery looked serious about was appreciating the blonde's figure.

And she would have to work with this man every day? How could she? She'd never felt comfortable around handsome men. Every time she tried to engage one in conversation, she stumbled over her words....

But that was before the experiment. She'd written to each of her subjects at least once before zeroing in on Mr. Serious, and in those responses she'd learned a few things. Maybe it was time she tested her education. Satisfied she had the situation in hand, Shea hefted her carry-on bag higher on her shoulder and headed straight for Reese Barrett.

"Excuse me."

Reese turned and found himself gazing into the darkest blue eyes he'd ever seen. Dark as the night sky with just a hint of starry sparkle. The owner of the stunning blue eyes was petite, blond and...stacked. She also smelled good enough to eat. He couldn't decide if the fragrance reminded him of sunshine on a spring day or some exotic flower. Not that it mattered. He couldn't have made such a monumental decision with his brain completely rattled. And, brother, was it. Looking at her made him forget what he was doing, drove all rational thought from his head. At least he supposed that was what was happening—he'd never experienced anything like it before.

Reese knew he was staring at her, and any second now he was going to recover and be embarrassed by his bad manners, but for the life of him he couldn't stop. The first clear thought running through his mind was that he felt as if he'd just been kicked by the meanest bull that ever came out of a chute.

"Excuse me," the woman repeated, "but—"

"Uh, sorry." He took a step back. "Am I in your way?" She was in his. In his way of breathing regularly, thinking normally. With considerable effort he forced his gaze away from her and back to the spot where Belle's friend had been talking to the ticket agent. She was gone. "Damn." He turned, heading for baggage pickup.

"Mr. Barrett?"

He stopped, turned back. The blue-eyed blonde knew his name?

"You are Reese Barrett, aren't you?"

"Yes, ma'am."

She held out her hand. "I'm Shea Alexander."

"You—you're, uh…"

"Is there a problem?"

Oh yeah, there was a problem all right. And it was Ms. Shea You-sure-as-hell-don't-look-like-I-pictured-you Alexander. Those eyes, deep enough for a man to drown in. And a sexy mouth and body… His gaze slid over lush curves that couldn't possibly be disguised by the expensive slacks and matching jacket of pale mist green. He hadn't realized until this very moment how long it had been since a woman had affected him so strongly. Maybe his luck had finally changed.

Reese grinned. "Not from where I'm standing." He reached for her bags. "Let me get those for you. I'm parked just outside the terminal."

"Thank you."

One look. That's all it had taken to wipe away her confidence. It was one thing to be glib on paper, particularly when most of it was fantasy. It was quite another when the situation called for one-on-one contact. Suddenly, whatever confidence she'd found through her experiment vanished like morning dew on a hot summer day.

Poise dwindling by the second, she fell back on the only solid ground she knew—her intelligence.

Just keep everything strictly business. Pleasant, but

*businesslike. Don't think about his looks or the way he
radiates masculinity like a steam heater in the middle of
winter. Don't think about what it might be like to be
wanted by such a man.* Good advice, great advice,
but she couldn't stop stealing glances at Reese Barrett.

Why hadn't Belle warned her? Why hadn't her
best friend prepared her for Reese's lean-hipped,
square-jawed masculinity when she knew Shea's
near phobialike discomfort in the presence of
handsome men? The answer, of course, was simple. If Belle had told her about Reese, Shea would
have run like a scared rabbit, which was exactly
what she wanted to do now. But she had promised
Belle, and she couldn't, wouldn't back out. Besides, she knew Belle was terribly fond of Reese
and had nothing but praise for his work and joy at
their friendship. How intimidating could he really
be?

Then she remembered Reese and Cade were
longtime friends and had even traveled the rodeo
circuit together. Maybe they were alike and that's
why Belle got along so well with Reese. She had
said her husband was a bit of a rogue, but that was
part of his charm. Maybe that's what she liked
about the tall cowboy walking beside her. Shea
had to admit he had a roguish quality about him
that was undeniably attractive. Lord knew, she
hadn't been unaffected when she first saw him.

If she was brutally honest with herself, *unaffected* was a mild word. She'd actually tingled with
a kind of unnamed anticipation. A desire…

Desire?

Was that what she'd felt? That flash of heat.

That sudden breathlessness. Oh my, she thought. Not an altogether unpleasant sensation. Oh my, indeed...

No. That was unproductive thinking. Business, strictly business. She should put her reaction down to biology, a much more comfortable arena and one she could handle. But a small voice warned her that Reese might not fall neatly into any category, and controlling the situation might be easier said than done. Still, she had to do it. Truthfully, what other option did she have? She was just no good at this talking, flirting, man-woman thing. Shea decided to keep the conversation to a minimum rather than risk making a fool out of herself the very first day.

They walked to where Reese had parked his pickup. "No, this stays with me," she said when he reached to put her computer carrying case in the truck's bed with the other luggage. He shrugged, helped her into the truck, and they started off for Sweetwater Springs.

After several minutes of silence, Reese nodded to the open expanse of seat between them. "You can set your bag on the seat if it's uncomfortable in your lap."

"Oh, uh, that's okay, Mr. Barrett, I—"

"Call me Reese."

"Very well...Reese." He smiled and she experienced that same breathless sensation she had when she first saw him. Only now she was much closer and the effect was more intense, to say the least. Inside the truck, the air thickened, and she found it difficult to breathe. She unbuttoned her

jacket, exposing the matching shell beneath it.
"Uh, is it much farther to the ranch?"

"Not much. Your first time out here?"

"Yes."

"May be a little boring after your busy life in
Austin."

"No, I...I doubt that."

Out of the corner of his eye, Reese watched her
fiddle with the strap of the carrying case. She was
nervous and he had the feeling it had something
to do with him. Why would a poised, highly intelligent and beautiful woman like Shea Alexander
be nervous around a ragged cowboy? At that moment she inhaled deeply and sighed, causing
the... Was that blouse under her jacket silk? Whatever it was, it clung to her like a lover's whisper,
outlining her breasts. She might be a genius, but
she was also all woman. Totally feminine from the
tips of her ivory pumps to her shoulder-length
honey blond hair, which was so thick he'd bet she
had a hard time making it behave. And speaking
of behaving...

What was he doing drooling over Shea Alexander, when not ten minutes ago he couldn't wait to
read a letter from Natalie? He should be ashamed
of himself. Still, he thought, glancing at Shea, it
was hard not to drool.

No, he wasn't going to do this. He wasn't going
to let hormones interfere with a working relationship that had to hold up for at least six weeks. He
owed that much to Belle.

Another glance at Shea Alexander told him it
wasn't going to be easy.

"So, WHATDAYA THINK?"

"About what?"

"Shea," Cade said. "What do you think of her?"

The four of them had just finished a delicious meal of Posey's infamous chicken enchiladas, and he and Cade were in the courtyard waiting for the ladies to join them.

Reese shrugged. "She's okay, I guess."

"Okay? She's a knockout. And did you hear her IQ?"

Hear it? He'd almost dropped salsa on his best shirt when Cade asked if Shea objected to telling Reese her IQ. She'd tossed out a ridiculously high number as if she were giving him the time of day. And when he'd asked if she knew anything about the hands-on part of a winery as opposed to strictly the business end, she'd rattled off a list of books she had read. Even quoted from some. Many of the titles Reese recognized and were, in fact, part of his personal library.

"All right, she's smart and easy on the eyes."

"And for a woman that got all of her knowledge of winemaking from books, she sure as hell knows her stuff." Cade grinned at Reese. "Better watch your step, partner."

Reese had to admit Shea had displayed an amazing grasp of producing and marketing wine. She'd asked some savvy questions about the winery, the growers, the business in general. And the whole time she had deliberately avoided looking at him. He knew, because he'd spent a good deal of his time stealing glances at her. If he didn't know that she was a confident, handle-any-situation businesswoman, he would have sworn she was as nervous as she had been when he picked her up.

"There you are." Belle and Shea strolled into the courtyard.

Cade took his wife's hand, smiling down at her. "Just waitin' on you, darlin'." He pulled her into his embrace, softly kissed her mouth. When the kiss ended, Belle gazed into his eyes for a second, then rested her head on his shoulder.

Shea couldn't stop staring. She'd read about it in books, seen it portrayed in movies, but until this very moment she'd never been in the presence of love. Real love. There it was right in front of her eyes. In the way Belle and Cade looked at each other, touched each other. It was physical and emotional, even spiritual. It surrounded them, radiated from them.

And filled her with a desperate longing for just a taste of what they had.

"I was going over some things with Shea as we came outside. In fact, I was just about to mention that her timing was perfect." Belle turned to her friend. "We have two important 'events,' I guess you could call them, that take place within the next ten days. The first is our field tasting, which happens day after tomorrow."

"Field tasting?"

Belle laughed. "That's our name for it. What we do is gather whatever winery employees and ranch hands want to participate, along with friends and neighbors, and do a tasting. Our marketing people are there with some questionnaires, but it's very informal and casual. I think you'll enjoy it."

"Oh, uh, I thought I'd told you...I don't drink."

Three pairs of eyes stared at her.

"You mean hard liquor," Belle said. "I know you weren't much for drinking when we were in college, but—"

"I don't drink anything anymore. A couple of years ago I, uh, discovered I was kind of allergic to alcohol." Allergic to making a fool of herself at the company Christmas party was more like it. She'd had two drinks and had all but thrown herself at the sexy vice president in accounting. She hadn't touched a drop since then. "Is that a problem?"

"No." Belle shivered slightly in the evening breeze. "Normally, Reese and I do the real tasting of the wine as it's fermenting and after, but of course, I'm avoiding alcohol because of the baby. This other is almost like a party and I thought you might enjoy yourself, but it's no big deal."

"I see. And the second event?"

"The annual growers association dinner dance," Cade told her. "It's about as close as we get to black-tie around these parts."

Belle shivered again and Cade hugged her to him. "You cold, darlin'?"

"A little. Think I'll go in."

Shea started to go, too. "We should all proba-bly—"

"Heavens, no," Belle insisted. "You stay. Visit with Reese. Starting tomorrow you'll be working together, so you should get acquainted."

With that, the McBrides walked into the house, leaving her alone with Reese.

Alone with tall, dark and rugged. Shea's calm

nose-dived. Great. Now what? "Please don't, uh, feel like you have to stay, Mr. Barrett—"

"Reese."

"Sorry. Reese. You're not obligated to—"

"Tell me something. Are you nervous about taking over for Belle, or is it something about me that makes you skittish as an unbroken mare?"

"You? No, I—"

"Don't encounter many half-breeds in your fast-paced, high-tech world, do you?"

Good grief! He thought her nervousness stemmed from the fact that he was part Indian? "You think... Oh, no... that has nothing to do... I mean, I never even thought... " Oh God, she was stumbling all over herself here. She had to make him understand without sounding like a total idiot.

"Please believe me when I say it's not you, it's me." Well, half a truth was better than none. "I want to do a good job for Belle. You see, she helped me out at a time when I desperately needed it." Shea raised her eyes to him. "This may sound silly, but I want her to be proud of me."

"Nothing silly about loyalty."

Shea sighed, relieved. "I'm glad you understand. I just didn't want you to think that I was apprehensive about your heritage."

He didn't know if it was the plea for understanding he'd seen in her eyes or the tenderness in her voice when she spoke of Belle, but he believed her. So, if his bloodline didn't bother her, why was she babbling? Maybe she had some self-imposed rules about dipping her pen in company ink. Well, that was all right with him. Actually, it made things less complicated, and he breathed a little easier knowing that was one hurdle he didn't have to tackle.

"I mean, as far as I'm concerned, you're just an ordinary guy— Well, what I mean is—"

"Maybe we should quit while we're ahead."

Thank goodness. She wasn't doing this very well. Maybe that's because she couldn't stop staring at him. It wasn't her fault he was nice to look at, compelling actually. When she saw him this afternoon from a distance, she'd thought his face looked sculpted. Up close it was nothing short of a work of art. All planes and angles conveying a kind of finite strength that was true beauty. His height and broad shoulders only added to the aura of power.

He slid his hands into his front pockets and watched her watch him. "You got any questions about the business?"

"Now?"

"Whenever. Anything you want to know, just ask. I'm never very far away."

She was curious why some determined cowgirl hadn't snapped him up ages ago, but of course she didn't ask. And the thought of him being close at hand was...unsettling. But at the moment she couldn't have said unsettling bad or good. "I'll remember that."

"Well," he said, stretching his shoulder muscles. "We start early so I guess maybe we better go in."

As they stepped onto the porch, she felt his hand at the small of her back. An unconscious courtesy, an old-fashioned gesture. Another reminder that she was no longer in the fast-paced world she knew and where she felt so in control. For the first time Shea began to understand that Sweetwater Springs was, as Belle had once described it, another world. She was out of her element in more ways than one.

"Thanks, Reese. I'm looking forward to working with you." There, she thought. Very pleasant, strictly business. Just as she planned.

"Might want to save the thanks. I'm going to run you ragged with enough procedures and information to make you long for one of your high-powered, multimillion-dollar number-crunching sessions."

It wasn't what he said, but the way he said it. With an undertone of resentment in his voice. She realized he didn't think much of her or her abilities. Maybe he felt Belle had crowded him out by bringing in a stranger when he knew the business literally from the ground up. And maybe the best thing for her to do would be to set his mind at rest.

"I hope you don't think that I'm here to usurp your authority in any way, Reese. You know, try to take over where I shouldn't—"

"I know what the word *usurp* means."

Great, now she'd insulted him. "I just meant—"

"Like I said, let's quit while we're ahead. And since we're talking about authority, I've got just enough to tell you that by the end of the day tomorrow you're going to be sick of the sound of my voice. In fact, it'll feel like we're joined at the hip. Think you can keep up?"

Well, he didn't have to be insulting right back, she thought. Men who jumped to conclusions usually did so as a defense. Reese Barrett might be a real hunk-a-hunk of burning love, but he was also oozing chauvinism out of every pore. She'd fought this battle before in countless boardrooms and managed to survive. In fact, she was a seasoned veteran. A fact Mr. Barrett would soon realize fully. "Oh, I think I can manage."

AN HOUR LATER, alone in her room, she removed her three letters from Mr. Serious and reread them, hoping it would help put everything back into perspective. His words were comforting, an assurance that one day she'd be able to deal with the Reese Barretts of this world. Lord knew, she'd made a mess of it today.

She was maintaining the correspondence with the other subjects in her experiment, but after his second letter, she realized Mr. Serious not only was more responsive but fell more into line with what she would have really wanted, if and when she started looking for a real relationship. The questions she worked into her letters were answered with a straightforward, no sidestepping honesty, yet at the same time there was a gentleness and respect that was clearly stated, albeit between the lines. Take the way he had described himself in his last letter. Average height, average build, with dark hair. Shea smiled, remembering a glimpse of his humor when he had offered that he would never be competition for Tom Cruise, but at least his looks had never frightened small children. He was, he wrote, just an average, ordinary guy.

Shea tucked the letters away in a drawer, hoping there would be more soon. She had contacted the magazine before leaving Austin and arranged for them to hold her correspondence until she rented a post office box. She didn't want the letters coming to the ranch. After getting into her night-gown and slipping beneath the covers of the big four-poster bed in Belle's guest room, she closed her eyes, wondering what Mr. Serious looked like.

A bit above average height. Probably six foot, she decided. Not short by any means, but she had to admit she really liked tall men.

Average build. That was fine, too. Of course, there was something to be said for a pair of spec-tacularly broad shoulders.

Dark hair. Was it a little too long, almost curling over his collar?

Just an average guy. Not a word she could ap-ply to Reese, that was for sure, and...

Good Lord, she must be losing her mind!

Abruptly, Shea sat up and turned on the light as if that might help dispel some of her dark, way-ward thoughts. She took a deep breath. "You're anxious about tomorrow. Only natural. New proj-ect. New skills to learn. You're wound up, that's all." More deep breaths. "Clear your mind and go to sleep."

She flipped the light off, gave her pillow a cou-ple of fluff punches and settled down. But it wasn't that easy.

"'Think you can keep up?'" she mimicked to the darkness. "I'll be sick of the sound of his voice, all right. And as for ever being joined at the hip with a sexist cowboy..."

A mental image of the two of them hip to hip—

naked and hip to hip—flashed through her mind, and heat coursed through her body. "Oh my."

Regardless of the source, something had happened to her today that she couldn't quantify or calculate. Something totally out of her realm of experience. As bizarre as it sounded for a woman of her age, she'd discovered she was a creature of desire. Sexual desire. That hot little image of the two of them flesh to flesh came out of nowhere and surprised her.

And scared her.

Her whole life, her very existence, was built around her intellect. Emotions were confusing, disquieting and…and, dammit all, downright terrifying.

"Stop it!" she whispered, yanking the covers up to her neck. What possible difference did it make? She would bet her next bonus she wasn't Reese Barrett's type.

With every ounce of willpower, she tried to visualize Mr. Serious, or any of the other subjects of her experiment. Instead, she fell into a restless sleep, her dreams filled with thoughts and images of a tall, rugged winery manager who was anything but average.

3

A CUP OF COFFEE in his hand, Reese stopped at the door to Belle's office when he glimpsed Shea poring over some files. "Bright-eyed and bushy-tailed, I see."

Shea looked up and almost gasped. She *had* to stop reacting like this every time she saw him. But it was hard to react any other way when the man practically filled the entire doorway and stood there looking like...well, like he belonged in the pages of *Texas Men* magazine. On the cover, as hunk of the month. Too bad his manners didn't match his looks.

"Good morning, Reese. If you're looking for Belle, she's stepped out for a minute."

"Actually, I was looking for you."

"Me?"

'Belle thought you might want a tour of the winery."

"But I assumed she would—"

"Nope. We try to keep her from wandering around too much. Conveyer belts, barrels being moved, boxes being loaded, forklifts in and out...." He shook his head. "Just not safe."

"Oh, I hadn't thought of it, but I can see where that might be dangerous."

"Notice I said 'try.' She's as hardheaded as an

Arkansas mule when she decides to do things her way."

Shea had to smile at his dead-on assessment. "Not exactly a shrinking violet, is she?"

"Not so you'd notice. Did you ever meet Belle's grandfather?"

"Caesar Farentino? Yes, at our college graduation ceremony. A charming man."

"He was also tough as boot leather when the occasion called for it, and tenacious as a pit bull when he wanted his own way. Believe me," he told her between sips of coffee, "Belle comes by her stubborn streak naturally."

"One can't very well deny one's genes." As soon as the words were out of her mouth, she regretted them.

"Sure you can. It just doesn't work."

"I wasn't referring to—"

He held up a hand to stop her. "We covered that last night, remember? Now, how about that tour?"

"Yes, I'd appreciate that very much."

They walked through the office and out into the winery. Within minutes, Shea understood perfectly Reese's concern for Belle's safety. The place was buzzing with activity. And noise.

"Welcome to Château de Bubba," Reese said with a sweep of his hand.

"Château what?"

That's just our way of not getting too big for our britches. Wine is the nectar of the gods, after all."

Shea smiled and nodded. Reese seemed to be doing his best to put last night's talk aside. The least she could do was match his effort.

Reese pointed to an open archway and a driveway that extended some fifty feet or more to a weighing pad. "Growers bring their grapes in trucks or big gondolas. They're weighed, the red grapes are separated from the white, then both go into a crusher-destemmer."

"I read about that. You handle the red different from the white."

"Yeah. White grapes go directly from the destemmer to be pressed. The red are only slightly pressed into what we call mush. It all sits in a tank for six to twelve days because—"

"All grape juice is essentially white, so the skin has to come into contact with the juice in order to make red wine." For Shea, knowledge was mother's milk. She'd grown up on a steady diet of information, so it was only natural for her to collect and process data.

His look said he was clearly annoyed. "That's right, and—"

"After the mush sits, it's pressed again. Eventually the pulp is discarded, right?"

"Right."

"And no one has ever come up with a use for the pulp, have they?"

"No." He guided her with a hand at the small of her back as he had the night before, only this time his touch wasn't so light. "C'mon. I'll show you the bottling process."

They made their way around two gigantic tanks containing juice from white grapes in the process of fermenting. An employee with a clipboard was reading a set of gauges and taking down information. "Checking sugar levels," Reese said, raising his voice to be heard over the whine of the forklift loading cases of wine near the rear of the building. They walked between two more tanks, stepping out into an open area where another employee was using a propane torch on a wooden barrel.

"He's toasting a barrel, isn't he?" Shea said, beginning to enjoy herself. "Actually burning the wood in order to flavor the wine."

"Yes. The one he's toasting is an American style made with white oak."

"You make your own barrels?"

He nodded. "For the most part. We also use a French style, which takes longer to make. Made from French white oak and flamed with an oak fire. More expensive."

Shea was so engrossed in watching the toasting that she didn't notice the dinner-plate-size drain in the middle of the concrete floor. The thin and absurdly high heel of her shoe went into one of the holes in the drain's cover and stuck, pitching her forward. The next thing she knew she was draped over Reese's arm as if they'd just "dipped" after a dance. Holding on to him, she stared up into his face, only inches from hers.

"Gotta watch your step." Slowly, as if he had nothing better to do for the next decade, his gaze moved over her face, down her body, then back to her face. Just as slowly, his lips curved in a devastating smile. "Those shoes work just fine in some fancy boardroom. Out here, they're dangerous."

Dangerous, Shea thought, staring into his dark eyes with their even darker fringe of lashes. That's exactly what he was—dangerous. Deliciously dangerous.

"Might want to try boots."

"Boots," she said, as if she'd never heard the word before.

"Maybe some jeans. We're not big on high fashion around here."

He had one hand supporting her back, the other on her hip. All she could think of was heat. Heat from his touch. Waves of it, right through the fabric of her skirt, the silk of her panties to her skin. So much heat, as if he were actually touching *her*.

"Hang on," he said.

As if she had a choice. If he removed his arm, she'd fall flat on her behind. Wouldn't that be a pretty picture. Not exactly what she had in mind for her first day. "Oh…" He moved his hand from her hip, sliding it over her calf, then down her ankle. "What are you doing?" she all but shrieked.

"Settle down." He pulled her foot out of her shoe, then set her upright. She stepped away from him so fast she almost lost her balance again.

"Oh." Feeling a little ridiculous for overreacting, she tugged her skirt down and tried to pull herself together. It wasn't easy, considering she couldn't have done a better job of embarrassing herself if she had tried. "Thank you," she said briskly, and turned to walk away.

"You'll need this."

She turned back and found herself eyeball to toe with her shoe. And there he stood, looking so stoic, or maybe *smug* was a better word. If she could have run away, she would have.

Instead she took a calming breath, slipped her shoe back on and cleared her throat. "Shall we finish the tour?"

He pointed toward the rows of aging barrels. "After you."

Talk about uptight, Reese thought, following her. The "thank-yous" had rolled off her lips easily enough, but they were courtesies, nothing more. Not a spark of warmth in those blue eyes. And what was that thing about him touching her leg? She couldn't put distance between them quick enough. He understood from Belle that Shea could whip up a billion-dollar business plan the way some people put a jigsaw puzzle together and make it look easy. Because of her genius, undoubtedly she was used to being treated with deference. The day had started off pleasant enough and she seemed congenial. For the life of him, he couldn't figure out why it had all gone south. But he did know she'd better lose the attitude. They were going to have to work together, and by God, he wasn't going to spend the next six weeks trying to defrost the ice queen.

AFTER LUNCH REESE STOPPED by Belle's office, praying he'd find her and not Shea. No such luck.

"Where's Belle?"

"She went home," Shea replied without looking up from the keyboard of her laptop. "Her back was really bothering her."

"Is she all right?"

The concern in his voice pulled Shea's attention away from the computer. "I think so."

"You're not sure?"

"Cade came by and she mentioned a twinge of discomfort. He immediately became concerned—

as you just did—and insisted she go home and get off her feet."

"Oh, well…good." For a second his heartbeat had shot from easy lope to full gallop. "She needs to take it easy."

"Exactly why I'm here. Is there a problem?"

"What?"

"You wanted to see Belle. Maybe I can help."

She hadn't been here a whole day, he thought, and already she was acting as if she could pick up where Belle left off? "Don't think so."

"I could try. Whatever the problem—"

"There's no problem. It's just that Belle always likes to take a look at the grapes as they come in, and visit with the growers. I guess you could come along if you want."

She thought about it for a second then shook her head. "No thanks."

"Why not?" he blurted, truly surprised.

"That's not my area of expertise."

"Not your area of… Excuse me, but I thought you were here to relieve Belle of some of her work-load and manage the business when she has the baby."

"Correct."

God, she sounded prissy. There was nothing he hated more than a prissy woman. "Then I don't…"

"Understand? Well—" She turned away from the computer, picked up a pencil and tapped it against her palm. "I am here to help with the business, but that doesn't necessarily mean every aspect. For instance, even though I may not know one grape from another, I do know management and—" she tapped the file lying open next to her computer "—I've already started working up some suggestions for cutting costs…"

"Cutting costs? Now, wait just a damn minute. Who gave you the authority to make changes?"

"Belle and I talked it over on the phone a couple of days ago. I guess she hasn't had time to discuss it with you."

"Obviously. But since you seem to be in the know, why don't you fill me in."

Great, she'd put her foot in it again. Damage control was needed, and quickly. "I really think Belle should be the one to discuss it with you. And I know she wanted your input before any changes were made. She, uh, realizes you and I have different approaches to doing business—"

He folded his arms across his chest. "You can say that again."

Shea cleared her throat. "For example, I enjoyed the tour you gave me this morning, but I must confess when you talked about marrying the vines, tending the soil and how good grapes produce good wine, I was lost. Fortunately, that *is* your area of expertise, so I'm not required—"

"Wrong." In two strides he was across the room. Leaning forward, his hands on the desk, he was almost in her face. "It doesn't make any difference if you're going to be here for six weeks or six hours, you have to know what you're dealing with. This business isn't like any other. Yeah, I like walking through the vineyards, putting my hands in the dirt, dealing with the growers, tasting the wines, quality control, marketing—the whole damn ball of wax. I like it because it's physical, and emotional, maybe even spiritual. Making wine is like making love—it's filled with passion, love and hard work. It doesn't come easy, but it's worth the effort."

Reese saw the shock in her eyes, followed by a look that was part fear, part...fascination. Almost envy. Bean counters, he thought. "Do you feel passionate about anything, Shea?"

"What?"

"You heard me." He leaned closer. "Passion. You know, intense emotion. Love. Sex."

All the color drained out of Shea's face. "I beg your pardon. That has nothing to do with—"

"Like hell it doesn't. Passion," he said, his voice low, husky, "has everything to do with everything. You have to be able to understand how wine is made to understand its value."

Shea pushed her chair back, hastily closing the file folder, and stood up. "I, uh, I'm sure you're right," she said, walking to the file cabinet.

Reese shook his head. "Beats me how a woman can look the way you do and not know about passion."

Appalled, she turned and faced him. "That is an outrageously sexist remark."

He shrugged. "I call 'em like I see 'em."

Shea opened her mouth to speak but couldn't. Finally she snapped, "I'm not sure I can work with you and your outdated attitude."

"Really? I thought you were a professional." Blue eyes sparked fire, but he ignored it. "I haven't said one thing in the last few minutes that wasn't gospel. You're the one who volunteered. This is a far cry from all those cold, unfeeling numbers you're used to handling." He moved closer. "We're more than profit and loss statements. More than ledgers. There's an intimacy about what we do."

Her back was up against the file cabinet. He knew it, yet he didn't stop. He closed the distance between them. "You're in over your head and you don't like to admit it."

"I—"

"Sink or swim time, Bright Eyes. If you really want to help Belle, you're gonna have to deal with all of it."

"Well, I—"

He was close enough to notice the pulse in the hollow of her throat was beating like crazy. "You don't strike me as a quitter."

"I'm not."

His gaze went to her mouth. "Good."

"I think, uh…I think we can, uh, work this situation out if we each give a little."

God, but her bottom lip was just about the softest-looking thing he'd ever seen. "I'm willing."

"And I, uh, think we should just keep this between us. You know, not worry Belle any more than necessary."

While his mind kept wondering how he could be so attracted to a woman who had to be told the definition of passion, his body had all the answers. "Agreed."

"Good. Oh, while we're setting ground rules, I'd like to make a request."

"Name it."

"I'd appreciate it if you didn't call me Bright Eyes. It's—"

"True," he said.

She cleared her throat. "I'll take that as a compliment, but it's also unprofessional."

He stared at her without answering for so long she had to squelch the urge to fold her arms in front of her in a purely protective gesture.

"Whatever," he finally said.

She wasn't quite sure that was a yes, but she didn't pursue it. "I'll, uh, wait to finish working up these figures until you talk with Belle."

"Probably best. I'd hate for you to waste your valuable time."

Shea took a deep breath. This was a no-win tug-of-war, and she decided discretion was, in this case, the better part of valor. "Do you think it would be possible for me to use one of the company vehicles? I'd like to run a couple of errands in town."

"Be happy to drive you since you're unfamiliar with the area and—"

"I'm perfectly capable of finding my way into Sweetwater Springs, Reese."

"All right. You can use my truck."

"Oh, no... I wouldn't want to inconvenience you."

He fished a set of keys out of his pocket and dropped them in her hand. "It's not a problem, Shea."

"Thank you. I promise I won't be gone long."

"Take as much time as you need. I'll be around when you get back," he told her, walking out the door.

She knew he probably thought it was strange that she wanted to go by herself. Well, he would just have to wonder, because her errands were none of his business. One errand, actually, and it was one she preferred that nobody, including Reese, knew about. She had to rent a post office box. How else could she continue her experiment?

"So, HOW WAS YOUR FIRST day?" Cade asked that evening at dinner.

Shea glanced at Reese. "Fine."

"I'm sorry I had to leave you in the lurch like that," Belle said. "Cade overreacted."

"The hell I did. Your back was killing you. It still is."

"I'm fine. Stop worrying."

Belle said it with a smile on her face, but Shea noticed she had adjusted her position in her chair several times. "Can I get you a pillow or something?"

"It's sweet of you to offer, but I don't need it. Really."

Cade snorted. "She's too stubborn to admit if she did."

"I'll second that," Reese said. "Think you're gonna have to hog-tie her to get her to take it easy, Ace."

"And don't think I won't. You know, it wouldn't hurt you to sleep late now that Shea is here."

"Golly gee." Belle fluttered her eyelashes. "What would we do without such big strong men to take care of us? And before either one of you big strong males answers, be warned. That was a rhetorical question."

"Maybe a little extra sleep would do you good, Belle," Reese put in, trying to suppress a grin. He got a threatening fork waved in his direction for his advice.

Cade leaned back in his chair, giving his wife a wicked smile and a loving look. "I'm tellin' you. She's developed a real mean streak."

"I can vouch for that," Reese said. "But seriously, why don't you sleep late in the morning if you want to? Shea was interested in seeing some of the vineyards—" he caught and held Shea's gaze as if to say, *Go along with me*, "—so I thought we could drive over to the O'Brian."

"All the more reason—" Belle shifted her position again "—that I should be in the office bright and early. Somebody has to prepare for the tasting."

"It's done. Besides, we moved it from morning to afternoon," Reese told her.

Belle glanced at the other three in turn. "I think there's a conspiracy afoot to keep me home."

"Not true," Reese said.

"Absolutely not," Shea agreed.

"Now, darlin', would we do that?"

"All right." Belle held up both hands in surrender. "I'll take the morning off. But..." she warned her husband, "I will be present for the tasting."

"Hey," Cade said to Reese. "We got the architect's drawings today for the changes we're going to make to the house. Wanna see 'em?"

"Sure."

"Back in a few minutes, darlin'."

"Take your time."

As soon as Cade and Reese were gone, Belle sighed. "I didn't want to say anything in front of Cade, but to tell the truth, it would be heaven to pretend I'm a lady of leisure for a few hours. Today hasn't been one of my better days."

Shea frowned. She didn't know anything about being pregnant, but she did know that both Cade and Reese seemed to be concerned. "Maybe you should call your doctor."

Belle shook her head. "I just saw him last Friday. I'm fine. The baby is fine. It's just that my back hurts a lot, which is natural…" She shifted again, and this time actually winced. "Damn, that hurts." She looked at Shea. "If you promise not to panic, I'll tell you something."

"What?"

"I do think the pain is getting worse."

"Belle—"

"You promised you wouldn't panic."

"I did not. Besides, it's too late. I'm calling Cade."

"No." Belle reached for her hand. "Just help me upstairs so I can stretch out on our bed."

"But—"

"C'mon. It's no big deal." She struggled out of her chair and started waddling out of the dining room.

"I still think I should call Cade," Shea insisted, catching up to her.

"Oh, he drives me—" Belle stopped, clutching her stomach. "Oh, no."

"What? What is it?"

"I…it really does hurt…." She turned frightened eyes to Shea. "Something's wrong. Too much..." Belle's knees buckled and she slid to the floor. "Too soon for the baby..."

"Cade!" Shea yelled at the top of her voice. "Oh God, Cade, come quick!"

Cade and Reese were there almost before she took another breath.

"Call 911," Cade ordered, taking Belle in his arms. Reese was already dialing. "Take it easy, darlin', everything's gonna be fine. I won't let anything bad happen to you or our baby."

Belle's whimpered response tore at Shea's heart and she looked at Reese. The fear in his eyes validated her own. While she half listened to him giving directions then calling the obstetrician, she turned back to Belle. Cade glanced up. "Shea, will you get a pillow and a blanket out of the bedroom?"

"Anything else?"

He shook his head and Shea raced upstairs to collect the items. By the time she got back down, Cade had Belle across his lap, rocking her like a baby. Sirens wailed in the distance, moving closer.

Within minutes the paramedics had arrived and were attending Belle. Cade didn't let go of her hand until he had no choice but to release her, as they placed her on a gurney for transport to the hospital.

As he climbed into the ambulance, Shea saw his face turn white when one of the paramedics commented, "Looks like we might have a premature delivery on our hands."

4

"DÉJÀ VU," Reese mumbled, his head down.

"What?"

Glancing up, he ran a hand through his dark hair. "Sorry. Just a few months ago Cade and I were in this same room, waiting to see if Belle and the baby were okay."

"You're referring to the accident not too long before they repeated their wedding vows," Shea said. "A fired employee was caught stealing and ran into her car when he tried to escape, didn't he?"

"Yeah. I didn't think Cade was going to make it. Never saw him like that before, or since. Until tonight."

Shea cast an anxious glance at the double doors that had swallowed the gurney carrying Belle less than a half hour ago. "They'll be okay. We just have to hang on to that thought. And Cade's with her. If there's any news—"

As if she had summoned him, the double doors parted and out walked a very weary-looking Cade. Reese and Shea rushed toward him at the same time. Shea opened her mouth with the first question, but Cade held up his hand to stop her. "Belle and the baby are both okay. For now."

"Is she in labor?" Reese asked.

"She was. They've stopped it for the time being."

"So, what happens now?"

"The doc wants to keep her here for a while. He says if she doesn't have any more contractions for the next twenty-four to thirty-six hours, he'll let her go home."

Shea put a hand on Cade's arm. He was trembling. Her heart went out to him. "That's good news."

"Yeah." He hung his head for a moment, and when he looked up, his eyes were misty. "She's been going up and down those stairs a thousand times a day trying to get the nursery just the way she wants it. I tried to help her, but..." He made a valiant effort to smile but wasn't completely successful. "You know Belle."

"Yeah." Reese, too, worked at a grin. "She'll do it her way or else."

Now that the immediate danger was past, Cade's tension needed an outlet and he found it. "I could just paddle her little butt. She has to do everything right when she wants to. Can't wait a minute. Hardheaded little..." He stopped, his gaze swinging from Shea to Reese, then propped his hands on his hips and sighed. "I haven't felt this helpless since Wizard threw me halfway across the arena then tried to tap-dance on my leg."

Shea had no idea who this Wizard was, but dancing on someone's leg sounded incredibly painful. At her bewildered look, Cade explained.

"A bull."

"A vicious, cowboy-hatin' bull," Reese added.

"Oh."

Cade massaged the knotted muscles at the base of his neck. "Yeah. And facing ole Wizard was a snap compared to this last hour."

"How about a cup of the sludge that vending machine tries to pass off as coffee?" Reese asked. When Cade nodded, he turned to Shea. "How about you? Cream and sugar or black?"

"Cream and sugar, please. Can Belle have visitors?" she asked as Reese walked away.

"Maybe tomorrow the doc says."

"Can I bring her anything? Nightgowns?"

"Guess so. I really hadn't thought that far. Thanks, Shea. Yeah, that's great. Whatever she wants, she gets."

"I don't know you very well, Cade, but you and I agree on one thing—nothing is too good for Belle."

Now he smiled in earnest. "She's the best thing that ever happened to me, that's for sure."

Me, too, Shea thought. "I can see that for myself."

Reese returned with the coffee. "Since I know you're not leaving here tonight, why don't you let me take Shea home, then I'll come back and keep you company."

"Thanks, partner, but I'd feel better knowing you and Shea are taking care of things back home."

"You sure?"

"Yeah. You know I'll call if anything changes. Besides, Shea's gonna bring some things in for Belle, so you'll have to come back tomorrow morning."

Cade turned to Shea. "Sorry to dump everything on you all at once, but you can depend on Reese to help with whatever you need."

"We'll be fine."

"Yeah," Reese said. "Don't you give it a minute's worry. Shea and I are gonna keep everything running smooth as silk. Isn't that right, Shea?" The look in his eyes all but dared her to disagree.

"Right. Smooth as silk."

AN HOUR LATER as they left the lights of Lubbock behind and headed for Sweetwater Springs in the pickup, Reese glanced over at Shea. "You okay?"

"I think so."

"Pretty damn scary for a few minutes, wasn't it?"

She pushed a lock of hair out of her eyes and sighed. "You're telling me."

"Thanks for backing me up. I know it'll set Belle's mind at ease. We just won't tell her we got off to a rocky start."

"I meant what I said."

"Yeah, you sounded convincing enough."

"No, I meant it. Belle's like a sister to me. I'll do anything, no matter how distasteful, to make this time easier for her."

"Including work with me."

"I...I didn't mean it like that."

"Exactly how did you mean it?"

"Look, Reese, I've got nothing against you personally—"

"Oh, I see. Just men in general. I'm not surprised." Miss Frostbite, he thought.

The remark stung. More than she expected.

More than it should have. Maybe that was the reason she felt a sudden yearning to give as good as she got.

"No. I work with men all the time. And because I do, I've learned how to keep business relationships strictly on a business level. I see no reason why working with you should be any different."

His hands tightened on the truck's steering wheel. "Oh, you don't?"

"No. It's not as if there's any danger of us becoming...involved. You seem to be intelligent and hardworking, and I'm sure some women find you devastatingly attractive, but...you're just not my type."

"Really?"

"Yes."

"Well...that works out just fine, because you're not exactly what I'm used to, either. I like my women a little more...flexible."

"Well then, there's no problem."

"Nope. Not a one."

No problem at all, he thought. She wasn't soft and yielding the way he wanted a woman to be. She wasn't gentle and sweet. Except for the gentle way her hips swayed when she walked, and he'd bet her lips were sweet as...

No. Shea Alexander wasn't anything like the women he was used to, he told himself. Then why did he keep thinking about her? Because she was beautiful. Because she had a terrific body. Because...he wanted her. Okay, it was sexual attraction. Biology, that's all. He could handle it. He would handle it.

Satisfied he had everything under control, he

made a mental note to write Natalie a nice long letter.

BY EIGHT O'CLOCK the next morning Shea was up, dressed and packing a small bag for Belle. Posey, the cook and housekeeper, was a big help, pointing out which toiletries, closet and chest of drawers belonged to Belle. Shea collected the necessary sundries, then opened one of the drawers in search of nightgowns. When she did, she spotted a beautiful creation of cream-colored silk. Carefully, almost reverently, she picked it up, the fabric cool and soft in her hands. She'd seen such nightwear in catalogs but never owned anything like it. It was a whisper of seduction, and the temptation to hold it against her body and imagine how she would look in it was too great. Holding a thin strap in one hand at her shoulder and resting the other hand across her midriff to keep the gown in place, she stepped in front of the full-length mirror.

"Oh my," she whispered.

The neckline was provocative. No, it went past provocative and straight to "come and get me— now." The waterfall of ivory silk pooled at her feet and the effect was glamorous, enticing and…meant for a night of wild sex. Her cheeks grew warm at the image that popped into her head. An image of herself wrapped in a gown of silk and a man's embrace.

Standing outside the door, far enough back not to be seen in the mirror, Reese simply stared. Posey had informed him Shea was almost ready to leave, and he'd come upstairs to hurry her along, but he'd never expected to see anything like this. How could anyone look so sexy and innocent at the same time? Part "little girl playing dress-up," part "gorgeous woman all grown-up." Without a trace of the prim and proper businesswoman. He liked her this way. Of course, if she knew he was watching her, she'd probably hide behind her deep-freeze attitude. Still...there was nothing frosty about the way she was right now. If anything, she looked too hot to handle.

Dangerous thinking, he reminded himself as he turned and walked quietly to the head of the stairs. "Hey," he called out. "Where is everybody?"

"Uh, just a minute." Hastily, Shea folded the gown up and stuffed it back into the drawer. "Be right down." She snapped the bag shut and hurried out of the room.

Reese was standing at the top of the stairs. "Well, I see you took my advice."

"What?"

He pointed to her jeans and what appeared to be a brand-new and very expensive-looking pair of boots. "Nice boots."

She glanced down, then back at him, the unexpected compliment momentarily throwing her. "Th-thank you. I bought them to wear to a company shindig last year. I'd forgotten how comfortable they were."

He took the bag she'd packed. "Good pair of boots is like a good marriage. Takes a little getting used to, but if they're made right, they'll last a lifetime."

She wasn't quite sure how to respond to such a

profound observation, so she simply smiled and followed him down the stairs. Minutes later they were on their way to the hospital.

A SMILING BELLE WAS propped up in bed talking to Cade when Reese and Shea walked into the room.

"How are you?" Shea asked immediately.

"I'm fine."

"Really?"

"Really. I have to admit it was a little scary for a while, but the doctor says I can probably go home tomorrow."

"*If* she takes it easy," Cade added.

"Well, Belle's got the roses back in her cheeks." Reese eyed his old rodeo pal and shook his head. "But you look like you've been rode hard and put away wet."

"He slept in that awful chair all night." Belle pointed to an uncomfortable-looking straight-backed chair. "Will you please take him home, feed him and make sure he gets some rest?"

"I'm not going anywhere."

"Yes, you are, Cade McBride. I'm not going to have you keel over just when I need you most."

"That's why I'm not leavin'. You need me."

"Of course I do, but—"

"Hey," Reese interrupted. "Round two. The bell's rung."

Cade brought his wife's hand to his lips. "Sorry, darlin'. But if you think I'm walking out that door until you're walking out with me, forget it."

Belle sighed, gazing at him lovingly. "What am I going to do with you?"

He grinned. "We're in mixed company or I'd

tell you. Why don't you hold that thought while Reese and I step outside and go over some ranch business."

Shea saw the look that passed between the two friends and was concerned things were not as good as Belle wanted them to believe. "You're sure you're all right?"

"Of course. And thanks for bringing my things," Belle said, spotting the overnight bag. "No telling what I would have gotten if it had been left up to Cade or Reese. You're an angel."

"It's the least I can do."

"So, how are you and Reese getting along?"

"Oh, just fine." But Shea didn't meet Belle's gaze. "Gorgeous roses," she said, sniffing the fragrance.

"Reese is quite a man, isn't he?"

"Yes." Shea busied herself rearranging several of the roses clustered together.

"I don't know what I'd do without him. He really is my right arm."

"I'm sure he's invaluable."

"And not too bad to look at, either, is he?" When Shea didn't respond, Belle tried again. "Is he?"

"Is he what?"

"Good-looking."

"I suppose. If you like the rugged, macho type—"

At that moment Cade and his rugged, macho friend walked back into the room.

"Reese," Belle said, "I'd like to go over some things before you leave. The firm contracted to design and maintain the Web site is—"

"Put on hold for the time being," Cade said in a tone that brooked no argument.

"But—"

"No buts. If you're so all-fired worried about everything Reese and Shea have got to do, say goodbye so they can do it."

"He's right," Reese said. "We'll see you tomorrow."

Shea had her own reasons for wanting to end the visit. She leaned over and kissed Belle on the cheek. "Don't worry about a thing." Then she followed Reese out.

Outside Belle's room, Reese stopped so quickly she literally ran into him.

"Whoa." He put his hands on her shoulders. "How are you at putting a bedroom together?"

She blinked. "Excuse me?"

"Between now and the time Belle comes home, you and I have got to turn the study downstairs into a bedroom."

"What?"

"Cade gave me my marching orders. Belle is not going to climb so much as one stair until this baby is born."

Her heart shot into her throat, and without thinking she put her hand on his arm. "Something's wrong. Reese, what is it? What did Cade tell you while you two were out here?"

"Nothing's wrong."

"You're sure?"

"Yeah. And we want to keep it that way. Belle's doctor wants her to get lots of rest. No stairs. And absolutely no stress. Cade is gonna ride herd on her, but that means you and I have got our work cut out for us. We're gonna have to do double duty at the winery and the ranch."

"I'll do whatever it takes."

He smiled. "That's exactly what I told Cade you'd say."

Until that moment, he hadn't realized he still had his hands on her shoulders. Or that she was so close. Close enough to feel the heat from her body, smell her perfume and admire the sparkle in those gotcha blue eyes of hers.

His touch was warm, strong. And he was close, so close she could hardly breathe, much less think of what she should say. Exactly the kind of situation her experiment was supposed to make easier, but instead, here she stood, mute.

Reese dropped his hands and stepped back. The woman was lethal to the male population, he thought. Didn't she know she had come-and-get-me eyes, a mouth that had been created for kissing and a body that was designed to drive a man insane? Drive *this* man insane.

He took another step back. "You ready to go?"

Shea didn't say anything. Her voice wasn't trustworthy, and for a moment she thought the same thing about her legs. Then, with great effort, she pulled herself together and nodded.

"Guess the first order of business is the bedroom," Reese said.

Great, Shea thought. For years she'd dreamed of spending hours in a bedroom with a handsome man, but this wasn't exactly what she had in mind.

5

"YOU CAN'T JUST SHOVE a sofa to one side and then move a bed into a room this size," Shea said, surveying the late Caesar Farentino's study.

Reese wiped the sweat from his forehead. "Why the hell not?"

"Because Belle won't have enough room to walk to the bathroom."

They had been working steadily for more than an hour to make the existing furniture work with the addition of a double bed, and basically, they'd gotten nowhere. Reese insisted Belle would want the desk and her grandfather's chair left exactly where they were, which made it difficult to reconfigure the room.

Shea pushed a damp lock of hair from her eyes. "You're sure this is what Cade wanted?"

"For a smart lady, that's not so smart a question. Would I be putting myself through this if the doctor hadn't told Cade that Belle had to take it easy? No stairs. No stress of any kind, remember?"

She sighed. "Okay, look. This is the only room downstairs that works for a bedroom, right?"

"Right."

"And you insist the desk and the chair stay, right?"

"Right."

"Then the sofa has to go."

"Now, wait—"

"You can't have both. Make up your mind."

Hands on his hips, Reese glared at her, knowing he was defeated. "All right, but if Belle wants to know who's responsible, I'm throwing you to the wolves."

She was hot, sweaty and totally out of her element, but she'd be damned if he knew it. "I thought cowboys always deferred to their womenfolk."

"Only in John Wayne movies." He flexed his knees and pushed up with his legs, lifting the sofa. In moments he had it out in the foyer.

"Okay, now what?" she said when he returned.

"First order of business—" he jerked his shirttails out of his jeans "—is to get rid of this before I burn up." Grabbing his Western shirt with both hands, he pulled, causing the snaps to give way in a series of pops.

Shea could only gape. "What are you doing?"

"I told you I was hot." At her stunned expression, he gave her a look that said, Get over it, lady. "You act like you've never seen a bare-chested man before."

"Don't be ridiculous," she said, wondering if seeing such blatant masculinity displayed in movies or on television counted. "I just wasn't expecting it, that's all." She tried not to look at his chest, she really did. But it was difficult to ignore that expanse of broad shoulders and well-toned muscle. So much smooth power. She forced her gaze to his face and attempted a smile. "Comfortable?"

"Yeah." His gaze didn't falter but went straight to her breasts. "I highly recommend it."

Shea cleared her throat. "What's next?"

Reese grinned. "Well," he drawled, "there are several answers to that question, but I don't think you're ready for most of them."

"Reese—"

"Next, we ask Posey to collect the dust bunnies that were hiding under the couch, then we'll go upstairs and tackle the bed."

Five minutes later, Shea and Reese stood on either side of Belle and Cade's daunting double bed. The antique, ornately carved rosewood headboard came at least to Reese's shoulder, and the footboard looked as if it weighed a ton.

"All I can say is, I'm glad it isn't king-size."

"No kidding," Shea said. "How in the world are we going to get this...this monster downstairs?"

"Take it apart, I guess."

"Can we? I wouldn't want anything to happen to it. It's probably been in Belle's family for generations. And even if it comes apart, I'm not sure you should be moving something that size all by yourself."

"I can handle it."

In the process of removing the comforter, sheets and pillows from the bed, Shea rolled her eyes. "That's testosterone talking. Why don't you get a couple of the ranch hands—"

"They're all busy, so you're stuck with a Schwarzenegger reject." In an obvious contradiction to his self-description, he yanked the mattress, then the box spring to the floor. He removed one end of the headboard from the side rails, then walked around and removed the other end. "Now, just hold it up for a minute—" he stepped into the empty space between the side rails "—until I unhook the footboard."

"Reese."

Head down, he tugged at the stubborn rail. "Hold on."

"Reese, I can't!"

Hearing the panic in her voice, he snapped his head around, then everything happened at once. Shea screamed, trying to avoid the crushing weight of the massive headboard as it fell.

Moving so fast he was almost a blur, Reese kicked the footboard out of the way, caught Shea in a diving tackle and, using his body as a cushion, rolled with her to safety. The headboard crashed but didn't break apart, landing not two feet from their heads. They lay in a tangle of arms and legs with Shea on her back staring up at him. He had one arm beneath her back, one leg hooked over hers.

"Are you all right?"

Blue eyes, wide with fear, blinked twice. "I—I..."

The trembling began in Shea's voice, moving through her chest, arms and legs like spring floods overflowing riverbanks.

"Shea? Are you hurt?"

"I—I—I'm not sure."

Knowing he'd taken the brunt of the fall, Reese was relatively confident she was in one piece. But better safe than sorry. He had to be sure. A hint of a smile tilted one corner of his mouth. She wasn't going to like this.

"Just lie still for a minute." He plowed his fingers through her hair, checking her scalp for bumps, then slid his hand down her neck, across her collarbone to one shoulder, then the other, skimming the swell of her breast.

"Wh-what are...what are you d-doing?" she whispered, her body tingling from the adrenaline rush and other sensations that had absolutely nothing to do with adrenaline.

"Making sure there's nothing broken."

"I don't...think..."

"Can't be too sure. We wouldn't want you to be laid up right along with Belle, now would we?"

He pushed her arm away from her body. His big hand coasted along her ribs from side to side, down over her hip, her thigh, stroking, probing...

"That's... I'm fine. You don't—"

When he took her chin in his hand, whatever she had intended to say drifted right out of her head. With gentle pressure he turned her head to one side, then the other. "Does that hurt?"

"No."

"Headache?"

"No."

He hadn't released her chin, and for a moment, she didn't think he was going to. For a moment, as she stared into his dark eyes, she thought he might, just might kiss her. But that was crazy. Why would he? She didn't particularly like him and was reasonably sure the feeling was mutual.

His eyes locked on hers. "Positive?" Slowly he withdrew his hand.

"Yes."

And his thumb skimmed her bottom lip.

Heat shot through her body. Her heart jumped, hammering in her chest like the anvil chorus. She was hot and cold, shaking and utterly calm all at the same time. If her body was out of control, it was nothing compared to her brain. Instinctively, she tried to analyze what was happening to her, but all her thought processes had either gone haywire or shut down completely. All that was left was feeling. And being surrounded by all that bare male flesh didn't help the situation. Her sight and senses were filled—no, overloaded—with Reese, bare-chested and so close she could almost feel his breath on her face.

She had to pull herself together before something—she wasn't quite sure what—happened. While she fought to regain her composure, Reese abruptly rolled away from her and got to his feet.

He flashed a grin and offered her a hand up. "I think you'll live."

One second she was on sensual overload, the next she was lying there looking up at him and his cocky grin. She'd never felt so ridiculous in her life. Worse, she would probably look like a klutz if she tried to scramble to her knees and get up on her own. Choosing the lesser of two evils, she took his hand.

"Thanks," she said when she was once again on her feet.

"Sure."

"No, I really mean it." She glanced at the rosewood headboard, realizing how close it had come to hitting her. "At the very least I could have been seriously hurt. You may have even saved my life."

"Don't think I'd go that far, but—" he shrugged "—you're welcome." He turned to survey the damage to the bed. "Looks like we lucked out all the way around. No broken bones, and the bed has a few scratches, but it's still in one piece. Whatdaya say we get this thing downstairs and put back together. I don't know about you, but I've got work to do."

"Yes. Absolutely."

It took them another hour and multiple trips up and down the stairs to accomplish the task. And in that time, they gradually worked their way back to the place they were most comfortable with— sniping at each other. Finally, everything was finished except to get fresh sheets and make the bed.

"Guess I'll leave you to do the finishing touches." He pulled on his shirt but didn't snap it. "You know, fluff the pillows, make everything look nice. All that female stuff."

Shea thought she might gag. "It's a wonder you're not appalled that your big strong friend actually sleeps in a bed like this."

"Who said anything about sleeping?"

She hung her head and mumbled, "I might have known."

"Excuse me?"

She looked at him. "Do you ever read anything other than wine industry newsletters or *Horseman* or *Playboy* magazine? The feminist movement may not be the topic on every man's lips in this part of the state, but I'm sure you've at least read about it."

"Bright Eyes, you'd be surprised what I read."

With that he turned and walked out, leaving her to do the "female stuff."

If there had been anything handy, heavy and replaceable, she would have picked it up and thrown it at him. Or at the wall, or at any place, person or thing that might help get rid of her anger.

"The man is infuriating," she muttered. "He treats me like a child."

Except for those brief few minutes today on the floor, her conscience insisted. She certainly hadn't felt like a child with his hands all over her. No, indeed. And for the first time in her memory, she hadn't felt capable of thinking her way out of a situation. She'd just felt. Period. All that tingling had come out of nowhere, hit her like a tsunami, washed her up on the shores of confusion and beached her. Logically, intellectually, she knew the label was sexual tension. Emotionally, personally, she had no idea it could be so powerful and... She touched her bottom lip, remembering the feel of his thumb sliding over her skin.

Exciting.

ANOTHER MINUTE OR TWO and he wasn't sure he would have gotten out of that bedroom alive, Reese decided. Not only had he enjoyed making sure Shea wasn't hurt, he'd actually considered doing some exploration while he was at it. Just exactly how soft were her lips? And what would she have done if he'd kissed her like he'd wanted to. And God, how he'd wanted to.

What the hell was wrong with him, anyway?

She wasn't his type. Yeah, okay, so she had a mouthwatering body. A man would have to be dead not to respond to that body of hers. And maybe there was a little hell-raisin' left in him, because he did enjoy seeing how far he could go, teasing her, tweaking her anger, even shocking her.

Of course, it had backfired on him.

Touching her might have started out as a joke, but it sure didn't end up that way. He hadn't been teasing when he held her chin in his hand or when he'd "accidentally" allowed his thumb to glide across her bottom lip. He'd be the worst kind of hypocrite if he didn't admit he wanted her, but he hadn't been only thinking of sex when he looked into her eyes. Something strange had happened, something almost…tender.

That's crazy, he told himself. *Get a grip, cowboy.* Take one well-built woman, add a normal, red-blooded man, a clinch and a tumble, and the result was bound to equal a lot of heat.

Yeah, heat. That's all it was.

To confirm his opinion, he reminded himself that she got right back to being bossy just as soon as she was on her feet again. The woman never backed off. And she was going to be here at least five more weeks.

She'd either kill him or drive him crazy by then, Reese thought, walking toward the ranch office. The only ray of hope was that with Belle out of the picture and Cade spending huge chunks of time caring for her, he and Shea would have their hands full trying to keep everything running smoothly. She would have to take care of more of the hands-on aspects of wine making. No more avoiding it because it wasn't her "area of expertise." She could start with the wine tasting tomorrow afternoon. And frankly, he didn't give a damn if she liked that or not. He wasn't totally wild about picking up the slack regarding ranch operations, but it had to be done. And it just might keep Shea out of his hair. An excellent idea, considering they couldn't get along for more than five minutes. He was even willing to share the blame for their lack of compatibility. No two ways about it, they just rubbed each other the wrong way.

As soon as the word *rubbed* came to mind, so did the memory of touching her mouth, wanting her. He shoved the memory aside, deliberately training his thoughts on his last letter from Natalie. Sweet Natalie. She was the kind of woman he needed. And the sooner he made arrangements to meet her face-to-face, the happier he would be.

Hang on to that thought, cowboy, Reese told himself.

THE NEXT DAY CADE BROUGHT Belle home from the hospital and Shea helped settle her friend in her new bedroom. Cade and Reese had their heads together in the foyer discussing something, and when they walked back into Caesar's office, it soon became clear Mrs. McBride intended on taking Mr. McBride to task for rearranging her life without permission. Shea and Reese knew when to make an exit and said goodbye.

Reese walked ahead of Shea, almost as if he had forgotten she was with him. Then he stopped suddenly. "Oh, I almost forgot. Here." He handed Shea a set of car keys.

"Your keys. But I don't—"

"Not mine, Belle's."

"Belle's?"

"Yeah." He started walking again, heading for his truck. "Cade gave them to me a few minutes ago. You can drive her Suburban while you're here. She sure as hell won't be needing it. From the sound of the heated discussion we just left, Cade's gonna have his hands full keeping her in that bed."

"She wasn't very happy, was she?"

"That's got to be the understatement of the decade. Don't know about you, but I'm glad I've got plenty to keep me away from the house for the rest of the day."

"Do you honestly think you'll get off that easy? As soon as she settles down, your phone will start ringing off the wall."

"She'll have to leave a message."

"You really don't want to talk to her, do you?"

"I haven't got time. In about five minutes, I'll be on my way to talk to one of the growers, then I'm going to the O'Brian ranch to take a look at a bull. That should take up the rest of the morning, and the tasting has been rescheduled for this afternoon. By the way, I expect you to be there."

"I'd like to observe—"

"Like hell. You're going to taste."

His tone was harsh, definite. "But I thought I made it clear—"

"That you don't like to drink. Well, don't worry, you won't *have* to drink. You only get enough to taste and you can choose to spit the wine out rather than swallow. But you're talking about a tablespoon of wine, for crying out loud. You really think we'd invite our employees and a few friends to participate in some kind of drunken orgy?"

"Of course not, but—"

"Then cut me some slack, dammit." He stopped, took a deep breath and turned to face her.

"Reese, I'm not trying to be difficult—"

"If you're not, you're giving a damned good imitation, and it's gotta stop." When she opened her mouth to defend herself, he held up a hand. "I need to talk to you and I need your promise that our conversation goes no further."

"Why?"

He raked his hands through his hair, and for the first time, she realized he wasn't angry. He was worried. "Because I can't have you running to Belle with this. It's about her and the baby." His gaze met hers. "I need your promise, Shea."

Suddenly she wasn't sure she wanted to hear what he had to say. She could see the concern in his eyes. "You have my promise."

"The doctors are worried. It seems Belle's developed high blood pressure. Seriously high. And then there's some kind of covering at the entrance to the womb that women lose right before they give birth. I don't know all the correct terms, but the doc told Cade if the mother loses it, then doesn't deliver for days or even weeks, there's danger of an infection. So Belle's got to stay in that bed. With absolutely no stress. She'll confine her exercise to trips to the dinner table and the bathroom. And she won't lift anything heavier than a glass of iced tea."

"Surely Cade's not trying to keep that information from her?"

"No. In fact, right about now he's telling her everything."

When she winced, he said, "Yeah, I know. After that he's gonna give her the list of restrictions and lay down the law about her following them. She's not going to like it, but she'll do it. You know Belle. When she puts her mind to something, it's Katy bar the door. She had a close call with that accident early in her pregnancy, and nothing is more important to her than having a healthy baby."

"Yes."

"Cade wants to keep her spirits up and he doesn't want her worried about the winery or the ranch. That means you and I are going to be working our respective butts off."

"I told you I would do whatever it takes to help Belle."

"Oh, one more thing. Normally, you would work in tandem with Belle, but that's no good now. If you have questions I can't answer, or you can't find me, go directly to Cade. He wants anything to do with business filtered through him."

"So she keeps her blood pressure down."

"You got it."

He was frowning so hard it looked painful, and Shea had an unexpected and amazingly powerful urge to put her fingers on his forehead and smooth the frown away. "She'll be all right, Reese."

"Yeah."

Shea glanced over her shoulder at the house,

thinking of the couple inside and the fears they must be facing. Then she remembered the overwhelming love she'd felt that first night. The presence of love. They had it in spades. They always would. She looked at Reese. "They'll make it together."

"They've got to." He, too, gazed at the house for a moment, then turned to walk away. "Gotta go. That grower's waiting. See you at the tasting. Two sharp."

Shea watched him leave and realized that for all his bluster and macho attitude, he cared deeply about his friends. Unless her ears deceived her, there was a tone of desperation in his voice when he'd said, "They've got to." Maybe there was a real heart beating under that tough exterior.

SHEA MADE IT A POINT to be in the conference room set up for the tasting five minutes early.

The long, rectangular table seated at least fifteen, and almost all the chairs were taken. Against the wall at the far end of the room stood three carts, two with various bottles of wine, the other with glasses and silver platters of crackers. Along the center of the table were more bottles and what she assumed were comment cards in front of each chair. As she made her way to an empty chair, she recognized a few of the winery personnel. A woman Shea guessed to be in her mid-thirties came toward her, smiling, and offered her hand.

"Hey, there. I'm Dorothy Fielding. I'm the secretary over at the ranch. You must be Belle's friend." They shook hands. "Glad to meetcha.

We're all just plumb tickled you're gonna help out. 'Specially now."

"Thank you."

"And we'll all pitch in and do our part," Dorothy said. "Don't you worry. You need anything at all, you just come see me."

Obviously, word of Belle's situation had traveled. Dorothy Fielding's offer was every bit as sincere as her smile. Not surprising, Shea thought. From what she'd seen, the winery and ranch employees were like a family.

Shea smiled. "I just may take you up on that, Dorothy."

"If you're lookin' for help, I'd be happy to volunteer."

"I'll just bet you would," Dorothy said to the attractive man who'd come to stand beside her.

"Shea, this is Luke Tucker, a ranch hand. Luke, say hello to Miss Alexander."

"Hello, sugar."

"Now, none of your sweet talk, Luke," Dorothy warned, then turned to Shea. "Just pay him no mind—"

At that moment Reese walked into the room.

Luke glanced at the manager, then smiled at Shea. "I'll catch you later, sugar."

As Shea watched Reese walk the length of the table, smiling, shaking hands along the way, she was reminded again that he was a big man. And not just in size. He radiated confidence when he entered the room. A man who knew who he was and where he was going.

He took a seat at the end of the table. Not at the head, which he certainly could have, but the end.

In the last few hours, she had seen several different sides to Reese Barrett. Interesting sides.

Smiling, Reese rubbed his hands together. "Well, now we get to the fun stuff. I hope everybody's had a nice big lunch and you're rarin' to go."

Shea wasn't sure what she had expected, but it soon became apparent that these field tastings, as Belle had called them, were very informal. Reese poured the wine himself and everyone shared their opinions. There was a lot of laughter. Determined to do her part, she took tiny sips from each glass, discovering that Reese had been right when he'd said tasters didn't get drunk. However, after sipping and discussing three or four different wines, she did feel more comfortable. After the sixth sample of wine, she even laughed at a joke Luke told, and was amazed to learn they'd been tasting for almost two hours. Where had the time gone? she wondered. She tried to keep all the labels straight in her mind, but soon names like Cabernet Sauvignon, Merlot Cellar Select, Chenin Blanc, Johannesburg Riesling and Signature Red and White all began to blur together. Not that it mattered. They all tasted good. In fact, they all tasted wonderful.

She had just finished a lively conversation with Dorothy on how to rate the rear ends of various movie stars and professional football players when she felt a tap on her shoulder. She looked up and found Luke standing beside her. "Oh, hello."

"Hello, yourself. Say, how 'bout you and me going to get some of the best Tex-Mex food in the state?"

"That sounds lovely."

"Don't know about lovely, but we can have a helluva good time. You dance, sugar?"

"Uh, well—"

"They got a little dance floor at this place and I'm just dyin' to move you around to a soft, slow beat."

"Tucker."

"Yeah." Luke looked up and found Reese standing next to them.

"Help Ramos bring in another case of the merlot, will you?" Reese said.

"Sure thing." Luke turned his attention back to Shea. "Get right on it just as soon as Miz Alexander and I finish makin' arrangements—"

"Think you better do it now."

"So that's the way of things, is it?"

"The merlot, Tucker."

Shea looked at the two men and wondered why Reese's dark gaze was so disapproving. Luke was just being friendly. Reese had wanted her to be friendly, hadn't he? Well, so, what was the big deal? she wondered. When she turned back to Luke to thank him for the invitation, he was gone. She stared at the empty space for a second, then confronted Reese.

"He dissdapeared."

"Yeah."

She tried to smile at him, but it came out lopsided. "You make very good wine, did you know that?"

"Did you have lunch, Shea?"

"Lunch?" She checked her watch and discovered she had to put a lot of effort into focusing. "It's almost dinnertime."

"Uh-huh."

"Posey's pancakes," she said.

"That was breakfast. What about lunch?"

He seemed to be obsessed with her eating habits for some reason. "Didn't eat."

"That's what I thought."

"I don't have to eat if I don't want to, thank you very much. Has anyone ever told you that you have a tendency to be bossy?"

"Uh-huh. C'mon."

"Wait." She might be feeling the effects of the wine, but she wasn't drunk. At least she didn't think so. And she was certainly nowhere near intoxicated enough to let him pull his take-charge routine on her. "Where are we going?"

"To get some food in your stomach."

She smiled as she stood up. "Oh, well, that's a good idea. Very nice of you. Is everybody going?" She glanced around the table and found they were alone. "Where'd everybody go?"

"Home," Reese said. "It's after five o'clock."

"Goodness gracious. That late? Well, we better go see what Posey's cooked up for dinner. You know, now that you mention food, I'm hungry."

"Good."

He led her out of the conference room, collected her purse and walked her out of the winery.

Shea fumbled for her car keys. "Ta-da," she said, dangling them in front of her. "We can go in my car. No, wait. That's Belle's car. Anyway, we can go in that big red thing." She pointed to a spot slightly past the Suburban.

Reese took the keys. "I'll drive." He helped her into the truck and closed her door.

As he was walking around to the driver's side, Shea shook her head. "Pushy. Very pushy. But a nice rear." When he was behind the wheel, she looked over at him. "Definitely a five."

"Am I supposed to know what the hell you're talking about?"

"A five. On a scale of one to five, your rear end is a five. Not a five plus, which would be like Michael Douglas or Troy Actman—"

"Aikman."

"Yeah. Him. But you're close. Very close. And definitely a five."

"I'm honored."

"You should be. I'm very precise in my comparisons. Very rarely do I make mistakes."

"I'll bet."

She peered out the window as they drove through the main gate to the ranch, down the driveway and past the house. "Where are we going?"

"My house."

"Okay."

Oh, brother, Reese thought. She was in worse shape than he'd suspected.

He'd first realized the wine was getting to her when he heard her laugh out loud at one of Luke Tucker's jokes. Luke was a good hand, but he had a well-deserved reputation as a ladies' man, and he was flirting with Shea bold as brass.

Reese didn't like it worth a damn. From that point on, he'd kept a close eye on her. In her "relaxed" mood, it wouldn't do for Luke to think he could take advantage of the situation. He told himself Shea might be used to fending off lawyers in thousand-dollar suits, but she had no idea how persistent a determined cowboy could be. Keeping an eye on her was the least he could do for Belle's best friend. It didn't matter to him one bit if she wanted to make a fool of herself. But she should know what she was dealing with.

Come to think of it, he'd never really liked Luke all that much. And when Luke made his play, Reese hadn't hesitated to step in and send the hand on his way.

Now he was doubly glad he had. Shea was definitely tipsy. Otherwise, she would never have been so nonchalant about being taken to his cabin. First order of business was to get some food into her.

He parked the Suburban and with a little effort was able to get her out of the truck and into the cabin. Slipping an arm around her waist for support, he stopped in the doorway and flipped on the lights.

"Oh my," Shea said. "You're a slob."

"It's the maid's day off."

"Oh well. That's all—oops." He tugged on her arm and she plopped down on his sofa.

"Just sit there and be quiet. I'll fix you a sandwich."

"Do you have wheat bread? It's really better for you, you know."

Reese grinned. He couldn't help it. She looked kind of cute sitting there, trying to act so prim and proper when she was practically three sheets to the wind. "I'll see what I can do."

A few moments later, in the middle of constructing a sandwich, he glanced over his shoulder and found her standing in front of his stereo equipment, flipping through a stack of CDs.

"I want to dance," she announced. "I never get to dance."

"Why didn't you ask Luke? I'm sure he'd be accommodating."

"Who?"

"Never mind."

"Still want to dance," she insisted.

"After you eat." Carrying her food, he grabbed her hand and tried to lead her back to the sofa.

"Do I have to?" she pleaded.

Oh, she was going to hate herself in the morning, "How about a deal? You eat a few bites, then we'll dance."

"Promise?"

"Oh, yeah."

She squinted her eyes at him. "I don't trust you."

"Now, there's a shocker. How about a compromise? One dance for one half of this sandwich. But the sandwich comes first."

"Oh, all right." She walked over to the sofa, flopped down beside him and held out her hand.

He watched while she ate the agreed-upon half and washed it down with milk. But when he tried to push the other half at her, she balked. "You promised."

Against his better judgment, Reese shoved a Garth Brooks CD in the player and hit the play button. Then he walked back to Shea, took her hand and pulled her into his arms.

His first thought was that she fit him perfectly. The second was slower coming, but a surprise.

She felt so damned good in his arms, he didn't want to let her go.

As if in agreement, she laid her head on his chest, sighed and snuggled against him like she wanted to stay there forever. He smiled, feeling as if he'd just won a contest and he was holding the prize in his arms. *Eat your heart out, Luke Tucker*, he thought.

Now who's taking advantage? his conscience asked. He'd seen red when Luke moved in on Shea, and now here he was, holding her close, knowing she was a little under the influence. This was no good. When the song ended, he would insist on her eating the rest of the sandwich. He figured within the next hour or so, she would begin to lose the pleasant buzz she was enjoying. And when it wore off, he was going to have one very upset, if not downright angry, woman on his hands. Too bad, he thought. Ten to one, tomorrow she wouldn't remember much of what happened. Or at least she'd claim she didn't remember.

Shea lifted her head and looked at him. "You're a good dancer."

"Thanks."

"No, really. Not that I'm any expert. I even missed my senior prom. But I think you're a good dancer."

"How come you missed the prom?"

"Nobody asked me. Did you know I taught myself how to dance? Got a video tape, a book from the library, and taught myself. I'm very smart, you know."

"I've noticed."

"Sometimes I'm too smart." She grinned at him. "But not tonight."

"Nope." He gave her a spin as the song ended and aimed her toward the sofa.

She stopped abruptly, turning to face him. "You were going to kiss me, weren't you?"

"What?"

She waggled her finger in his face. "Aw, c'mon, admit it. When the bed fell, you thought about kissing me, didn't you?"

"Guilty as charged."

"Aha! I knew it. Why didn't you?"

"I didn't think you'd appreciate it."

"Then why don't you kiss me now?"

"Shea—"

"Chicken."

Reese laughed. "I sure hope you're able to find your sense of humor tomorrow."

"Why?"

"You're gonna need it."

"No. Why don't you kiss me?" she insisted.

"You've had too much to drink. I don't take that kind of advantage."

"Even if I give you permission?"

"Especially if you give me permission. Your judgment is slightly impaired at the moment."

"I'll bet what's his name would have kissed me."

"Luke?" Reese snorted. "He'd probably do a lot more than kiss you. With or without your permission."

"Think so?"

Reese stared at her and couldn't believe she was

actually smiling. She was playing him against Luke and enjoying every minute of it. His patience went up in smoke, and his temper snapped.

"You're cute, Bright Eyes." He put his hands on her shoulders, turned her around and all but shoved her down on the sofa. "But you're not my type."

Reese regretted the words the instant they were out of his mouth. He regretted them even more when he saw the pain flash across her eyes. He sat beside her and handed her the plate holding the rest of her sandwich. "C'mon, Bright Eyes. You'll feel better when you finish this. And trust me. Tomorrow you'll be glad I didn't kiss you."

She gazed into his eyes for several moments, then took the plate. In a voice barely above a whisper, she said, "I think I'm already glad."

6

HE FELT LIKE A HEEL. A first-class son of a bitch. And he'd been feeling that way for the last twenty minutes with no sign things were going to get better any time soon. Not while Shea was sitting on his sofa becoming more sober by the minute.

He had left her alone to finish eating and gone to the kitchen. Making a show of cleaning up, he stretched the time as far as he could. How many more times could he wipe the countertop without looking like a fool?

A jealous fool.

It took him a few seconds to recover from the shock before he realized it was true. He'd been jealous that she had even thought about kissing Luke Tucker. Any man would have reacted the same way, he tried to convince himself. No man wants to have a woman in his arms one minute, and her mentioning another man the next. A man had his pride, after all. But it was more than pride and he knew it. If there was one thing he hated, it was for a woman to play a man for a fool. Worse, playing two men for fools. God knew, he'd seen it enough times traveling the rodeo circuit.

And he'd been a part of that kind of triangle one too many times.

Not that tonight was a similar situation, because

he certainly had no designs on Shea. The situation just triggered some old hurts, that's all. It had nothing to do with Shea. She was too argumentative for his tastes. Too bossy and way too prissy. Shea Alexander was as different from the kind of woman he wanted, a woman like Natalie for instance, as day from night. Thinking of Natalie, he realized he had been intending to respond to her last letter for several days, but ever since Shea arrived, all his time had been taken up showing her the ropes and trying not to lose his footing in their power struggle.

Yeah. That's what this was about. Power, not jealousy.

He'd just tripped over one of his weaknesses and his ego got a little dented. So what? Really, when he thought about what had happened, he was actually trying to protect Shea. Satisfied he had everything settled in his mind, he left the kitchen to make his much needed apology.

"Shea—"

"I think I'm ready to go home now." She stood, pleased that at least her voice sounded strong. "I don't want to inconvenience you any further."

"You're not. Shea, listen—"

"No. I'd rather just leave. If you don't think I can drive Belle's truck back around to the front of the house, then I'll walk. One way or the other, I'm leaving."

"We'll both walk," he said, opening the door for her.

Once outside, Shea breathed in the cool night air. It cleared away the last of the cobwebs left behind by the tasting. She would be fine now. All she had to do was make it to the house and she could go to her room and cry about making such a fool of herself.

The house was almost a quarter of a mile from Reese's cabin and they walked along in silence for several minutes. Finally, he put a hand on her arm and stopped her.

"I'm not letting you go inside until I apologize."

She didn't look at him. "You have nothing to apologize for."

"I was rude."

"Actually, you were just being honest. It's laudable."

"Will you stop trying to let me off the hook? I hurt your feelings and I'm sorry. It's just that when you asked me why I didn't kiss you, then mentioned Luke probably would have…Well, let's just say I thought you were being coy."

"Coy? Me?"

"Yeah. And I won't tolerate a woman playing one man against another."

"Me? You thought—"

"I let my prejudices control my mouth. You were a handy target, and I'm sorry."

She stared at him. "I can't believe you thought I was trying to be coy. Even when I asked why you didn't kiss me?"

He glanced at the ground. "That could have been part of your game."

"Somebody…some woman really cut your heart out, didn't she?"

Reese's head snapped up. "No. I've still got my heart." Slightly ragged, he could have added, but still intact. "I'll just make damn sure the next woman I give it to is trustworthy."

"And subservient?"

"What?"

"That's what you want, isn't it? A woman who thinks you're wonderful."

"Well, sure—"

"That your every opinion is gospel. And thinks equality of the sexes means wanting sex as often as you do."

"I never said anything of the kind, and—"

"Of course you did, only not so bluntly. Let's face it. You're a normal red-blooded man—"

"Damn right, but—"

"And you admitted you thought about kissing me when the bed fell apart. But you didn't."

"Yeah."

"And why not? Because I'm not your type. I've definitely got my own opinions. No one's words, with the possible exception of the apostle Paul, are gospel. And as for equality, your definition and mine are light-years apart." She raised both her hands as if in surrender. "I rest my case. I'm not your type. That is to say, I'm not—and never will be—an eyelash-fluttering, ego-flattering bubble brain. Therefore it *was* a waste of time to pursue kissing me."

"That's the craziest logic I've ever heard. If I didn't know better, I'd think you wanted me to kiss you."

She glared at him.

"Well, did you?"

"Did I what?"

"Want me to kiss you?"

"Yes."

"Why the hell didn't you say so in the first place?" he all but shouted, pulling her into his arms. His mouth came down on hers in an anything but gentle kiss.

She wasn't sure what she expected. Maybe the same kind of heat she'd experienced when they were tangled together on the floor. What she got wasn't just heat but a blast of white-hot power. Explosive power. Her whole body tingled, anticipated...what? Her one experience had left her totally unprepared for this kind of kiss, this kind of stunning pleasure.

No one was more surprised than Reese. And the instant her lips touched his, he knew he was in trouble. Just the feel of her mouth on his obliterated every thought from his mind, except for the way she tasted, soft and sweet. With a deep-throated groan, he pulled her closer. Moving one hand down her back, pressing her hips to his, he tangled the other hand in her hair, holding her captive for his greedy mouth. And it was greedy, desperately so. His mouth took hers from every delicious, arousing angle. It should have been enough. It wasn't. The more he took, the more he wanted. It was possession, pure and simple. He wanted to possess her, but at the same time he wanted her strength, her independent spirit to meet him on equal ground. A small part of his brain, which had managed to escape the testosterone storm whipping through his body, instinctively knew such a meeting would be beyond anything he could imagine. In trying to prove her wrong, all he'd succeeded in doing was proving her right to a degree he'd never dreamed possible.

Shea wound her arms around his neck, drawing him closer, but it wasn't close enough. Her head was spinning, swirling. She was out of control, and for the first time in her life, she gladly surrendered, exchanging power for pleasure, knowing she was getting the best of the deal. Coiling her arms more tightly around his neck, she brought her body into intimate contact with his, then moaned from the sweet heat of pleasure. The kiss got hotter. Heads angled, mouths ground against each other, tongues mated.

They both reached the incendiary point at the same time, but Reese was the first to break the kiss. Gasping for breath, stunned at the potency of the kiss, they simply stared at each other.

When Reese released her, she took a step back.

"Shea—"

"Why?" She wasn't sure if she was talking to him or to herself. Why had he kissed her? And why had she wanted him to, knowing she wasn't what he wanted?

Because she wanted him. She wanted Reese Barrett. Desperately. Sexually.

He took a step toward her and she took another step back. "Why...why didn't you...kiss me while I was drunk?" she whispered. "It would have been so much simpler." With that, she turned and ran to the house.

Reese let her go, mainly because he didn't have the vaguest idea what he would have said if he caught up with her. What the hell had just happened? One minute they were arguing—par for the course—the next they were practically eating each other alive. He shook his head. Talk about the earth moving. He'd never kissed or been kissed like that before. Who would have thought there was so much passion beneath that no-nonsense, straitlaced veneer? And speaking of passion, he couldn't deny he'd wanted Shea like hell on fire. Not that he was a stranger to desire, but this was something…different, a kind of deep-seated craving he'd never experienced before.

Accustomed to being in control, Reese wasn't sure he liked the idea of Shea, or any woman, having such a powerful effect on him. It was a damned good thing she wasn't his type or…

Or what?

What might have happened if they'd taken the kiss to its logical conclusion? Would he have pulled her to the ground and made love to her right there like some mindless primitive? Because primitive was sure as hell a good description of how he felt, what he wanted. Truthfully, it was a good thing she stepped away from him when she did. Although for the life of him he couldn't understand the bizarre logic in her last words.

Why didn't you kiss me while I was drunk? It would have been so much simpler.

"Crazy," he muttered to the dark as he turned and headed back to his cabin.

Reese shoved his hands into his pockets. He was not looking forward to tomorrow. If Shea had been determined to get and keep the upper hand in their little tug-of-war before, she'd be worse now. Oh yeah, tomorrow was going to be a real lulu.

SHEA WOKE UP with a headache, but it had little to do with the amount of wine she had consumed last night.

Last night.

A memory crowded the fuzzy edge of her mind. A memory of her insisting Reese...dance with her? Followed closely by a vision of her in his arms while music played. "Great. You begged the man to dance with you, then draped yourself all over him like crepe paper on a homecoming parade float. Just peachy."

She groaned, rolled over in bed and yanked a pillow over her head. Oh, no, she thought. Not again.

What was it with her and booze? She couldn't believe she had acted so outrageously. And with Reese! One thing was for sure: she simply couldn't drink and that's all there was to it. In fact, she should probably wear one of those Medic Alert tags, specially designed for her. *Warning: Alcohol makes this woman stupid. Not allowed to consume alcohol in the presence of attractive males.*

Disgusted with herself, she sat up in bed, drew her knees up and ran her hands through her hair. "Oh God, just how big a fool was I last night?"

Another memory popped into her head, and this time there was nothing fuzzy about it. It was startlingly clear. Reese, his mouth on hers. Her arms around his neck urging him closer. And the kiss...

"Oh, n-o-o-o." Her head fell forward onto her knees. Now she knew for sure how big a fool she'd been. Huge. Mammoth. Astronomical. It would have been so much easier if he had kissed her when she was inebriated. Then she could have claimed she didn't remember the silly kiss. But she couldn't claim that now, and in truth the kiss had been anything but silly.

It had been wonderful. The stuff of dreams. Granted, very erotic dreams, but dreams, nonetheless.

And she *had* asked him to kiss her. There was no way to avoid that little slice of truth. Thinking back, she realized she had wanted him to kiss her as they lay tangled in each other's arms after the bed fell. But, of course, she managed to convince herself it would be crazy, that she didn't even particularly like him, when in reality…

Ah, yes, reality. Shea's world was built on reality. The reality of hard facts, proven theories, profits in this column, losses in that column. Her reality left little room for emotions. Well, here's reality for you, she thought. She wanted Reese Barrett, macho attitude and all. It didn't make sense, and she knew nothing would ever come of it because of the very reason she'd given him last night.

She wasn't his type.

"Men don't make passes at girls who wear glasses." She quoted one of Marilyn Monroe's lines from *How to Marry a Millionaire.* "Or have genius IQs," she added.

Same song she'd heard most of her life, only this time it hurt more than ever before. More than she'd thought it possible to hurt. And now she had to drag herself out of her room, out of her self-pity, and face Reese. Right this minute she could think of a thousand places she would rather be.

"Maybe I could just pack a bag and head for

Mexico. I could always send a sombrero as a baby gift."

Even though the idea had momentary merit, she knew it was ludicrous to think about leaving. Belle needed her.

With a sigh of resignation, Shea got out of bed and headed for the shower. Okay, she thought, letting the warm water soothe her nerves. How was she going to handle this situation without making it worse? Apologize to Reese? The whole idea of groveling made her want to throw up. He would gloat. She just knew it. And why wouldn't he? For a man like Reese, seeing her reduced to a simpering female had to be the ultimate I-told-you-so opportunity. No. She couldn't apologize. It would be the final humiliation.

She couldn't pretend she was drunk and had no memory of the kiss. They both knew better. She would just have to tough it out.

Forty-five minutes later she was dressed and on her way to the winery, ready to face Reese. She hoped.

BY NINE-THIRTY SHE WAS a nervous wreck. Where was he?

"He's probably letting me sweat, chewing my fingernails to the quick waiting for him to show. The jerk."

By ten-thirty he still hadn't shown. Shea had given herself a hundred pep talks, trying to prepare for the minute he walked through her door, none of which she could remember now. In sheer frustration, she pulled out the winery's tax file.

She would bury herself in deductions and hope for the best. She didn't have to wait much longer.

"Good morning," Reese said from the doorway a few moments later.

Shea's head snapped up and she dropped her pencil. "G-good morning."

"Sorry I wasn't here earlier, but I had some ranch business to attend to."

"Oh, no problem. I didn't even realize you were out," she lied. "I've had my nose buried in IRS deductions."

"Taxes, huh?"

"Yes. Very complicated."

"And you didn't even notice I wasn't around."

"No. Should I have?"

Reese just stared at her. "Well, if that don't beat all," he said.

"Pardon?"

"Here I was, worried you might be embarrassed about the fact that you kissed me last night, and—"

"I kissed you? I think you have that backward."

"Not from where I was standing."

"Y-you were the one doing the kissing."

"At your request."

Shea swallowed. As bluffs went, it was pretty weak, but it was all she could come up with. "All right. I admit that I'd had too much to drink—"

"Hold it. You're not going to try that old 'I was too drunk to remember what happened' routine, are you? Because if that's your plan, you can forget it." He walked to the desk. "You asked to be kissed and I was only too happy to oblige. After the first contact, I don't think either of us cared who was kissing who. Let's just call it a draw, shall we?"

"Thank you." She couldn't believe he was letting her off the hook, and so quickly. "That's very gentlemanly of you."

He propped a hip on the corner of her desk. "You know, I've been thinking about what you said."

"What did I say?"

"That it would have been simpler if we'd kissed while you were drunk."

So much for letting her off the hook. "I thought we called it a draw."

"Then you could have said you didn't remember, right?"

"Do you always close a topic, then open it again?"

He leaned toward her. "I agreed there was equal participation on both our parts. I didn't say anything about dropping the subject."

"Look," she said in her most professional voice. "Last night we kissed. I've been kissed before, and I'm sure you have, too. It didn't mean anything—"

"Oh, it didn't?"

"No. It didn't mean anything, and it never should have happened. Wouldn't have happened if I had been—" she almost said "in control" "—myself. I suggest we forget it and get back to business. This is an office, after all."

He couldn't have said if it was pride, bruised ego or that troublesome little devil on his shoulder that prodded him to pursue the topic when he knew he was treading on dangerous ground.

"And you like it when everything is strictly business, right?"

"I don't see anything wrong with—"

"No emotions, right? Messy things, emotions. I've tangled with them a time or two myself. It's easier to run—"

"I beg your pardon? I'm not running anywhere. And I think this discussion is at an end." She closed the file, got up and walked to the filing cabinet. When she turned around, he was right in front of her.

"So, my kiss meant nothing, huh?"

"I'm sorry if that puts a dent in your oversize ego."

"You didn't even like it, right?"

"Well—"

"Tell me you didn't like my kiss and we'll forget the whole thing."

"I didn't—"

"Liar."

"Now, just a minute—"

"The truth, Shea." He came closer, so close they were almost touching. "All I want is the truth."

And the truth would leave her more vulnerable than she'd ever been in her life. Reality, she reminded herself. Reese was a dream. Better to lie than hang on to a dream she could never have.

"Reese, it was nice. And I admit that maybe the idea of flirting with a cowboy has a certain appeal. But if you're waiting for me to melt at your feet, I'm sorry. It's just not going to happen."

"Oh, it's not."

"I wouldn't worry about it." She plastered on a bright smile. "I'm sure there are lots of ladies dying to melt at your feet. Now," she said, putting a hand on his arm and moving him aside as if he were no more substantial than a breeze, "if you'll excuse me, I've got work to do."

Reese stared at her, torn between wanting to strangle her and wanting to grab her and kiss her senseless. She was lying. He knew it and so did she. The way she'd gone all hot and wild in his arms last night was no pretense. Nobody was that good at acting. She couldn't admit that she enjoyed it every bit as much as he had. Her denial chilled him like a cold sweat. Temper simmered. If he didn't get the hell out of here right now...

Her back to the door, Shea jumped when it slammed. She didn't even realize she'd been holding her breath until then. He was mad, of course. She'd nicked his pride and that was unforgivable. Well, his pride would heal. She wasn't so sure about her heart.

Shea turned and looked out the window at the parking lot in time to see Reese slam the door to his truck, much as he'd done to her office door a moment ago. The truck shot out of its space, screeched to a halt, then took off out of the lot and onto the road leading to the ranch. With any kind of luck, she thought, he would be gone the rest of the day. And she'd be able to pretend she didn't miss him.

Dust billowed out in a cloud a quarter of a mile long as Reese drove his pickup like a bat out of hell. He hit the brakes, almost spinning into the driveway beside the house, then barreled on toward the round pen. He ground the truck to a halt, got out and slammed the door.

"Cade!" he bellowed.

"Yo" came the response from inside the round pen.

Cade McBride glanced up from cooling down a horse he was training just as Reese stalked into the enclosure. "Hey there, partner. What's—"

"I'm beggin' you. As my best friend, you've got to help me."

The horse jerked at Reese's disquieting tone of voice. "Whoa, boy." Cade soothed the animal, then turned to his friend. "What's goin'—"

"Let me come back to work at the ranch. Assign me to ride fence along the far north corner. I'll do it for a year. If you can't do that, fire me, or just put me out of my misery and shoot me. But don't make me work with that…that calculator dressed up like a woman."

When Cade motioned, a groom came over and relieved him of the nervous horse. "Now," he said to Reese, "what the hell are you talking about?"

"Shea."

"What's wrong with Shea?"

"Oh, nothing much. She's just the bossiest, most hardheaded woman it's ever been my misfortune to run across. She's one big contradiction from horn to hoof. She can analyze and calculate like a computer and kiss like the hottest temptress since Eve."

"You kissed Shea?"

"She'd like to believe that, but the truth is, she asked for it."

"Asked for what?"

"Telling me it didn't mean a thing. What a little liar. She was kissing me back so hard I couldn't breathe. And let me tell you something. The next time I kiss her, it'll damn well mean something—"

"Reese!"

"What?" he yelled.

"You're outta the chute, partner, and the whistle's blown. Cool down before you blow a gasket. Now, take a deep breath and tell me what this is all about."

"Shea."

"I got that much."

"Cade, you've gotta do something."

"Sounds to me like you've already done something."

"What?"

"You kissed her."

Reese pointed his finger at his friend. "She kissed me right back."

"Uh-huh. You askin' my opinion?"

Still breathing heavily, Reese put his hands at his waist. "Yeah."

"Sounds to me like you got the hots for the lady from Austin."

7

"YOU'RE CRAZY."

"Am I?"

"I just said so, didn't I?"

"Hey, don't shoot the messenger. Just because you happen to be attracted to a beautiful woman is no reason—"

"I'm *not* attracted to her."

"Then why did you kiss her?"

"She asked me to."

"And since when have you complied with a woman's wishes if you didn't want to?"

"What are you talking about?"

"I'm talking about Reese Barrett. Single-minded, lives life on his own terms, lone wolf. When did you start doing *anything* you didn't want to do?"

"Great, I came to you for help and all you're giving me is more flak."

"All I'm saying is that if you weren't interested, she could have asked you to kiss her till the cows came home and it wouldn't have done any good. Besides, I saw the way you looked at her across the dinner table the first night she was here."

Calmer now, Reese shrugged. "No sin in looking."

"Absolutely not. I plan on indulging in a few

harmless glances myself between now and the time they pray over me."

"Just because she's pretty doesn't mean..." Reese thought for a moment, tempted to tell Cade about his pen pal, then shook his head. "She's just not what I had in mind."

"For what, a bed partner?"

"Hey, watch it. Shea's a lady."

Cade grinned. "And who says ladies don't have the same urges we men do? I happen to be married to a lady with a capital *L*, and I can tell you from personal experience...well, I could, but I won't. You'll just have to take my word. Belle's a lady from the ground up and more than enough woman for me."

Reese had the good grace to be embarrassed. Considering Belle was one of his best friends, that was more information than he needed. "I'm not so sure about Shea. She's strictly business." His hand sliced through the air in a gesture of finality.

"And you want a soft-spoken woman who will stand beside you through thick and thin, looking to you for strength and guidance, letting you make the decisions."

Standing near the gate to the round pen, Reese leaned against the rail. As much as he hated to admit it, Cade's description sounded a little too much like the one Shea had outlined. "Wouldn't put it exactly like that. Maybe someone more like Belle is what I had in mind."

On the other side of the fence, Cade burst into laughter. In fact, he laughed so hard he had to hang on to the rail for support.

"Would you tell me what's so damned funny?"

Reese asked when Cade finally got control of himself.

"Are we talking about the same Belle? Belle Farentino McBride, my wife?"

"Of course. She's smart and beautiful. Kind and loving, but not afraid to stand up for what she believes. And she loves you to distraction, though God knows why."

"Would you listen to yourself? Everything you just said about Belle applies to Shea, too. Except for lovin' me, of course. Why do you think she and Belle have been such good friends for so many years? They're—alike."

Reese opened his mouth to refute the statement, then closed it. He stared at Cade, trying to figure out just where the conversation had taken a wrong turn. Shea like Belle? How could that be? "But I don't argue with Belle," he said almost to himself. "We work great together."

"Now. But be honest. It wasn't that way in the beginning, particularly when Caesar was alive," Cade reminded him. "Just like Belle and I went head-to-head at first. As a matter of fact, every once in a while we still fight like a couple of cats in the same bag. And you see where we ended up."

"But Shea isn't anything like—"

"The woman you thought you wanted?"

"Yeah."

"Welcome to the club. You've known me most of my life. Would you have believed I'd end up with a woman like Belle? Or that I would have agreed to a marriage in name only?"

"Not in this lifetime."

"There you go."

"You fought it, that's for certain."

"Like a sinner at the gates of hell. At first, anyway. Even took off to Denver because she made me mad."

Propping a booted foot on the bottom rail of the fence, Reese grinned, remembering the rocky start to the McBride marriage. "She ran you off the place with a shotgun."

"But I came back."

"I always knew you would. You never welched on a deal in your life."

"That's not why I came back," Cade admitted. "I didn't have any choice."

"What do you mean?"

"Couldn't stop thinking about her, wanting her. I knew I wasn't good enough for her, but she got to me. See, I'd never been in love before, so I wasn't sure how I was supposed to feel. I came back to find out."

"But how did you know?"

Cade shrugged. "Simple. The more I was with her, the more I wanted to be with her, to take care of her, protect her. Not to mention the fact that I couldn't stand the idea of anyone else touching her. When I was finally able to see the truth, I knew it was never the land that enticed me into the marriage, it was Belle. It had been Belle all along. I was just too stubborn to admit it."

"You never mentioned any of this before."

"Well, hell, Reese. What'd you expect me to do? Invite you over for afternoon tea and spill my guts?"

They both laughed at the image Cade painted. "Of course, it took a bit of doin' to convince my darlin' Belle. She fought her passionate nature. Thought it left her too vulnerable. Took a while, but when she finally decided to take a chance on this old cowboy, she bowled me over."

Cade put a hand on Reese's shoulder. "There's something you need to remember about women like Belle and Shea."

"And that is?"

"They're as stubborn as we are."

"Tell me something I don't know."

"Well, I'll tell you this. You owe it to yourself to find out if that kiss was more than a passing fancy. And if Shea is more woman than you bargained for."

Maybe Cade had something, Reese thought, walking back to his truck. Maybe it was time to see if the reason Shea had gotten under his skin had more to do with attraction than he realized. But how did he find out when she acted like a bear with a sore paw every time he was around her?

Reese smiled. Most bears loved honey.

SHEA DROVE into Sweetwater Springs and went straight to the post office, hoping she would find something from *Texas Men* in her box. After her confrontation with Reese that morning, it would be wonderful to deal with men on a less personal level. To her delight there was a package. She walked out into the breezy late-afternoon sunshine, then crossed the street and sat down on one of the many benches situated around the courthouse square. Eagerly, she ripped open the large manila envelope, turned it upside down, and out poured several letters. But she had to make a quick grab when the insistent breeze almost blew her mail out of her hand. She tucked the empty envelope under her arm as she riffled through the letters.

All of her test subjects had written except Mr. Serious.

A letter from him would have gone a long way to restoring her confidence, she thought. He wrote to her about his love of the land and how he longed to find a meaningful relationship. She always felt so...happy after one of his letters. She could sure use a few happy feelings right now.

Disappointed, Shea stuffed the letters into her purse, deciding she would read them when she was alone that night. As she stood up, the wind whipped the envelope from beneath her arm, sending it tumbling across the courthouse lawn. Shea gave chase, caught up with it as it wrapped itself around the leg of another bench, but she wasn't quick enough, and it blew off again.

"Oh, damn." For half a second she thought about giving up, but knew she wouldn't be able to walk past the litter barrel with the slogan Don't Mess With Texas painted on the side without feeling guilty. The envelope evaded her again, sailing right into a gathering of three elderly men sitting on a bench beneath a huge oak tree. One of the men stomped on the wayward wrapper, ending the chase.

"This yours, ma'am?" he asked, jerking the paper out from under his boot.

"Yes, thank you." All three men stood.

The man holding the envelope tipped his hat.

"Alvin Delworthy, ma'am. And this here's Smitty Lewis and Old Walt."

"Gentlemen." She nodded to each of them. "Nice to meet you."

"Say," the one called Smitty said. "Ain't you that lady friend of Belle McBride's from Austin?"

"Yes, I am."

"We heard you was gonna help out. Mighty nice of you. Can't beat a good friend and that's a fact," Old Walt commented.

"Yes. Well..." Shea hated to be rude, but she couldn't stand around talking all day, and Alvin Delworthy seemed to be in no hurry to hand over the empty wrapper or offer to trash it himself. "Thanks for helping."

"Happy to oblige." Smitty grinned his toothless smile. "We seen you come outta the post office and seen the paper go a-flyin'. Wind comes across the caprock like a chargin' bull sometimes."

"So I noticed. Well, thanks again." She held out her hand for the envelope.

"Oh, yeah," Alvin said, as if he'd forgotten his catch. He glanced at the return address label with *Texas Men* stamped in bold print, then glanced at Shea.

Her cheeks were beet red. They had to be if the flush of heat she felt was any indication. "Uh, thanks again, and goodbye." Quickly, she took the envelope, folded it a couple of times and crammed it into her purse as she walked away. Speculation about the contents of the package would probably spice up the three old guys' spit-and-whittle conversation for days.

"One embarrassing episode down and one to

go," she said, wondering how she was going to face Reese at dinner that night. She could just see the look on his face when Belle asked how the tasting went yesterday.

Maybe she could fake a headache. She might not have to fake it considering the tension she experienced every time she was around Reese. Even now, remembering the way she had thrown herself at him last night, she felt a little sick to her stomach. How far off was a headache?

"Coward," she mumbled, backing the Suburban out of its parking space and heading back to the winery. "Absolutely gutless. Telling him you weren't going to melt at his feet. What a lie. You were a foot-deep puddle from the instant his lips touched yours, and you know it."

But knowing it and doing something about it were two different things. She'd skated by this morning because she had the element of surprise on her side. She couldn't expect to get away with that trick twice. Her lack of knowledge about how to handle a man hung around her neck like an albatross. She had to see this through and that was all there was to it. She couldn't run away. Couldn't hide. That left meeting the situation head-on.

"Not my first choice," she said, driving along Highway 87. She glanced at the letters stuck in the side pocket of her purse. "But then, experience was what I wanted. I just didn't expect it to be so... hands-on."

Her inexperience was bad enough, but last night had definitely compounded the problem. She still couldn't believe she had asked Reese to kiss her. Or, more amazing, that he had.

"Don't be silly. He probably felt sorry for you."

But it wasn't pity she'd tasted on his lips. In fact, she'd had a hard time deciding just who was kissing whom before it was over. Not that she had been capable of any kind of decision with his mouth moving on hers, yearning, demanding. Or with his arms holding her tight, making her feel so desired. Or with that breath-stealing, mind-robbing heat consuming her. She'd never known anything like it. As clichéd as it sounded, she could have sworn the earth moved, fireworks exploded, and she went spinning off the edge of the world. But whatever romantic frills she had attached to the kiss last night, they quickly vanished in the cold light of day.

The truth was, she'd had her first taste of plain old-fashioned desire. And she liked it. She liked the burst of fire and need, the wildness. It wasn't logical, and she had to admit it was a bit frightening. But it was also wonderful.

Of course, it wouldn't, couldn't happen again. Not with Reese, anyway. Logically, she knew that and accepted it. If you didn't count the tiny impulse to say, "What a pity."

As she pulled into the driveway of the ranch, she spotted his truck. *Be cool*, she told herself. All she had to do was keep up the front she had established this morning. Keep telling herself what she had told Reese—last night didn't mean anything.

"Yeah. And if you say it enough times, maybe you'll begin to believe it."

Shea sighed, climbed out of the truck and went inside. She walked straight to Belle's bedroom, pleased to find her looking relaxed and rested.

"A couple of days in bed did you a world of good." Shea said. "You look great!"

"I feel really good. And I probably should be ashamed of myself for allowing Cade and Posey to wait on me hand and foot, but it's too wonderful to refuse."

"Then don't. They love you, so let them pamper you. Where is everybody, by the way?"

"Reese is out with Cade. We bought a new bull and they're looking him over."

"Oh," Shea said.

"He gave me sort of a progress report on you. Not that I needed one."

"Did he?"

"Yes. He said he was amazed at how quickly you picked everything up. Said you joined in the spirit of the tasting yesterday and fit right in with everyone."

Shea could only stare at her friend. She couldn't believe Reese had lied.... On second thought, it made perfect sense. He didn't want Belle to think there was any dissension between two of the three people she depended on to run her business. He was only looking out for Belle and the baby. The guy might be a candidate for macho man of the year, but he cared about his friends. At least he had one redeeming quality.

"That was very generous of him."

"I think you impressed him."

"Oh, I wouldn't go that far." Not unless you defined "impressed" as "dented."

"No, really—"

At that moment they heard male voices in the

foyer. Shea squared her shoulders, prepared to smile and play the part Reese had given her.

The two men walked in. Reese stopped just inside the doorway and didn't say a word. Cade went straight over to his wife and gave her a kiss. "Hey there, darlin'. I was just tellin' Reese he should take Shea on a tour of the ranch."

Reese was probably planning on taking her out and staking her to an anthill, Shea thought, avoiding his gaze. Wasn't that how his ancestors used to get rid of their enemies?

"How does that sound to you, Shea?" Cade asked.

"Well, uh…"

"You do ride, don't you?"

"I, uh—"

"If she doesn't, I'll teach her."

Shea's head snapped around. Reese was staring at her, the look in his dark eyes indefinable. If he was still angry, he was doing a good job of keeping it hidden. "Uh, no… I mean, no, that won't be necessary. I know how to ride."

"Good," he said abruptly.

"I'll be glad when I can ride again." Belle patted her tummy.

Sitting beside her on the bed, Cade covered Belle's hand with his. "And I can teach little whosit to ride."

"Fine way to talk about your son—"

"Or daughter," Cade added. They smiled, gazing into each other's eyes, almost oblivious to the other couple.

"Well, I think I'll go upstairs," Shea announced, and started to slip out of the room.

"And, Reese," Belle said. "Y'all don't stay out so long you tire her out. Don't forget the dinner dance tomorrow night."

"Wouldn't dream of it." Reese followed Shea, his boot heels tapping on the Mexican tile floor as he walked.

When she got to the stairs, she turned to face him. "Look, I know you only offered to take me riding to please—"

"How long has it been since you've been up on a horse?"

"I belonged to a riding club until a couple of months ago, but—"

"Nine o'clock tomorrow morning okay with you?"

"Yes, but—"

"Oh, yeah. Wear a hat. That fair complexion of yours won't last long around here." He turned, heading for the door.

"Wait!"

He stopped, slowly turned back and waited.

"Uh…" She tried to think of a reasonable excuse to decline—other than the fact that she wasn't sure she wanted to be alone with him. "What about the winery?"

"It'll survive for a couple of hours without us."

"Oh."

Without another word, he turned and walked out of the house.

THE NEXT MORNING, dressed in jeans, boots and a long-sleeved blouse and carrying a hat borrowed from Belle, Shea headed for the kitchen. She decided to forgo breakfast since her stomach was turning handsprings, but a cup of coffee might help fortify her before Reese arrived. The sight that greeted her didn't do a thing to calm her stomach or her nerves.

Reese was standing at the counter filling two mugs with coffee when she came in. She looked fresh, sweet and sexy as all get-out. And nervous. His own confidence level might be sagging a bit, but he knew one thing for sure. He wanted to forget about coffee and riding. He wanted to forget about everything but stealing another taste of Shea's lips. He figured with that kind of want, he'd eventually find the confidence he needed.

He walked across the kitchen and handed her a cup of coffee. "Morning."

"Thanks. Good morning."

"You hungry?" She shook her head. "Sure? There's a whole pan full of Posey's biscuits on the stove."

"No, thanks." She held up her cup. "This is fine."

He claimed a tall bar stool, sat down and sipped his coffee, watching her. And watching her.

Shea's nerves were frayed. After their confrontation yesterday, she knew he was only being polite to her for Belle's benefit. "Reese, I, uh… This isn't necessary."

He didn't say anything, just silently sat there, regarding her. "I understand that we need to keep up appearances in front of Belle. Maybe Cade, too. But we don't have to continue the pretense when it's just the two of us. I know you don't like me very much—"

"I never said that."

"Well, after yesterday I thought—"

"That was yesterday."

"I don't understand."

"Let's just say you're dealing with a different man today. The new and improved Reese Barrett. Think you can handle that?"

New and improved? What did that mean? "Uh, sure."

"More coffee?" She shook her head. He poured himself another cup, seemingly in no hurry to leave.

"Do we, uh…do we have a particular direction, or are we just going to ride where our fancy takes us?" Shea asked, trying to make conversation.

"Some of both. We're headed to the O'Brian ranch on an errand. It's about three miles from here."

"Three miles? They live on Farentino—I mean, McBride land?"

"No. Even though their property is about the same size as this ranch, the adjoining section of their land is shaped like a big slice of pie. Their house, situated right at the point of the wedge, makes them our closest neighbors. Cade purchased a bull from Case O'Brian and I'm delivering the check."

"I see."

"So, tell me about this riding club."

"Oh, it's nothing special. My company sponsored a polo team. I played a little, then sort of lost interest."

"Polo, huh?" Very competitive, he thought, not the least bit surprised. She probably kept scores and stats for all the players in her head. Both teams. "So, three miles isn't too far for you?"

"Not a problem."

"Good." Reese knew damned good and well that even if it had been, he would be the last to hear it. He drained his coffee cup. "Ready to go?"

"Lead on."

He smiled. "My pleasure."

As Shea followed him out of the house and walked with him to the barn, she wasn't sure about this new and improved Reese Barrett. With the old one, at least she knew where she stood.

Reese saddled Belle's horse, Dolly, for Shea, and a gelding named Skedaddle for himself.

Shea patted Dolly's neck. "What a sweetheart you are."

"As long as the sun's shining," Reese said.

"What does the sun have to do with it?"

"Old Dolly here is gentle as a lamb until it storms. She doesn't like being penned up when there's thunder and lightning. Makes her crazy. She's busted down her stall once or twice to get free."

"Don't worry," he said, seeing her looking at the cloudless sky. "The weatherman isn't predicting rain until late tomorrow or the next day. And even that's a guesstimate." He swung himself up into the saddle and off they went.

As soon as they were away from the barn, Reese urged his horse into a lope. Shea had no difficulty staying up with him. She had almost forgotten the delicious sense of freedom only horseback riding can bring, and soon she was relaxed and thoroughly enjoying the ride.

OCCASIONALLY REESE pointed out a mesa or small canyon, giving their names, but basically they rode in silence. The three miles flew by, and within an hour they passed through the gate of the O'Brian ranch. As they walked the horses up to the house, a tall, attractive man who looked to be in his early fifties came out on the porch. He smiled.

"You didn't tell me you were traveling the old-fashioned way," the man said as they dismounted.

Reese shook his hand. "Case, this is Shea—"

"No need to tell me who this is. Most folks around here already know you on sight, Ms. Alexander. I'm Case O'Brian."

They shook hands. "Mr. O'Brian—"

"Case, please. And I didn't know how pretty you are or I'd a been over to introduce myself sooner."

"He kissed the Blarney stone and it took."

Shea looked up to see a younger version of Case O'Brian stepping onto the porch.

"My son, Devlin. Dev, meet Shea Alexander."

Devlin O'Brian walked straight to Shea and took her hand. "A real pleasure."

"Hey, Dev," Reese said, not particularly thrilled with the way O'Brian was looking at Shea. "I didn't know you were back."

O'Brian was a lady-killer with smooth good looks and an even smoother line. He'd traveled all over the world, and even though he'd never been a sailor, Reese would bet next month's paycheck he had at least one girl in every port.

And he was still holding Shea's hand.

"Got home day before yesterday," he said, never taking his eyes from Shea. In fact, he gave her a long, lingering once-over. "Now I wish I'd arrived sooner. Why don't y'all come inside and have some iced tea?" He tucked Shea's arm in his, turning toward the house as if it were all settled.

"Oh no, we wouldn't want you to go to any trouble."

"For you, no trouble at all."

Shea felt the smile Devlin O'Brian flashed her all the way to her toes. A smile, she decided, that was probably calculated to have just that effect. Charming, she thought. Very charming.

"That's very kind of—"

Reese stepped into their path. "Sorry. We can't stay. Maybe another time."

Shea blinked at Reese's abruptness. He was definitely the most unpredictable man she'd ever met. One minute he was smiling and friendly, the next he was curt and ill-mannered.

Devlin O'Brian turned to Shea and gave her another award-winning smile. "Too bad," he said. "I'm flying to Alaska tomorrow or I'd sure like to get better acquainted, Shea."

Reese didn't miss the way he used her first name. And the son of a bitch was *still* hanging on to her hand. "Yeah. Dev's a real globe-trotter. Never hangs around here for long." While he took an envelope from his shirt pocket and handed it to Case, he maneuvered himself alongside Shea. He put his hand at the small of her back , moving her away from Dev. "Well, guess we'd better be heading back."

Stunned and slightly embarrassed at Reese's

rudeness, Shea deliberately walked ahead of him. "It was nice to meet you, Case. And Dev."

Reese helped her mount Dolly, then he climbed on Skedaddle. "Pleasure doin' business with you, Case."

"Same here. Say hello to Cade and the lovely Belle."

"Will do." Reese turned his horse toward the gate, then looked at Shea. "After you."

They had just rounded a stand of live oaks that put the O'Brian ranch house out of sight when Shea reined Dolly to a halt. She was livid.

"Whoa." Reese brought his horse to a stop. "What's wrong?"

"Wrong? I can't believe you would even ask that question. What's wrong is your manners. New and improved, my fanny. You were rude to Devlin O'Brian."

"Rude?" He looked truly shocked. "I was rude? The man was all over you like a cold sweat and you call me rude?"

"He was not."

"He was practically drooling."

"He was very charming."

"Don't make me laugh. I've known Dev all his life. He turns on the charm the way some people turn on a water faucet."

"Well, it's too bad some of it didn't rub off on you." She dismounted and started walking, leading Dolly behind her.

"What are you doing?"

"I need to walk. Do you mind?"

Reese dismounted, caught up with her and grabbed her arm, but she pulled away. "As a matter of fact, I do. First you ask me to kiss you. Then you tell me it was nothing. Didn't mean a thing. And today you stand there and let a total stranger paw you."

Shea's mouth fell open. "That is so untrue. He was holding my hand."

"Given half a chance, he'd have done a lot more than hold your hand."

"What is that supposed to mean?"

He couldn't believe her naïveté. For a woman of the world, she sure asked some dumb questions. Reese shook his head. "You figure it out." He picked up Skedaddle's reins. Now *he* needed to walk.

What's to figure out? Shea wondered. Devlin O'Brian had only smiled, held her hand, looked deep into her eyes.... Slowly, it dawned on her what Reese meant. Surprised, she went racing after him.

"He was coming on to me?"

"Hell, yes, he was coming on to you. And you were lapping it up. Of course, it's no skin off my nose. You're past the age of consent."

Seeing her smile at Dev, when all he got was haughty glances, seeing her allow Dev to touch her so familiarly, when she denied his kiss... He'd be damned if he was going to tie himself in knots over a woman who would just as soon spit in his eye as look at him, no matter how...

Jealous?

No matter how jealous he was?

Dear Lord, he was.

He wanted Shea to smile at *him*. He wanted to

be the one holding her hand... Hell, he wanted her
warm and willing in his arms, in his bed.

"He was so smooth about it, I didn't even sus-
pect."

"Yeah, well... he's had a lot of practice."

"So you were just trying to protect me?"

"Something like that."

"I suppose I owe you an apology."

"Forget it."

"No, I—"

"Shut up, will you? Just shut up so I can do
this." His hand went to the back of her neck as his
mouth came down on hers.

After an instant of surprise, Shea responded out
of pure instinct, an instinct she hadn't even known
she possessed until he kissed her the first time.
That instinct was now working on all eight cylin-
ders, making her body hum. His mouth was
greedy. Hers was greedy right back. The kiss consumed her, crowding out everything else. All that
was left was ruthless desire. And desire, she had
discovered, was a power better shared.

He couldn't get enough of her. Not just the way
she tasted or felt. He couldn't get enough of *her*.
Wanting her closer, he pulled her hard against
him until her breasts flattened against his chest.
And still it wasn't close enough. The urge, desperate and deep, to be so close they were inseparable
was so powerful it was frightening. No woman,
Reese thought, taking the kiss deeper, had ever
felt this right in his arms. Sweet. Right. His.

Shea's heart beat a wild rhythm, as wild as the
need pulsing through her body. Never in her
wildest dreams had she thought it could be like

this. That she could want like this. And wasn't it just her luck that Reese would be the man to stir all these feelings in her. He wasn't anything like the man she imagined she wanted. But he was everything she needed.

"I—I'm confused," she whispered when they broke the kiss.

"You're not alone." His lips trailed down her throat.

"I didn't think we liked each other." The last word was practically a sigh.

"I know." He nibbled on her earlobe and she moaned.

"But—"

"I changed my mind."

She buried her hands in his hair, curled her fingers in the thickness. "Yesterday you said—"

"I said a lot of things yesterday." He rubbed his mouth slowly over hers. "So did you."

"You were waiting for… " His hands slid down her back to her hips, pressing her to him. "Oh, mmm…me to melt at your feet."

"You got the melting part right. Only I don't want you at my feet. I want you in my bed."

8

HE HAD MADE one hell of a mess out of things.

Reese stood in front of his office window looking out at the new vineyard being planted and couldn't work up any more interest than he could for the gathering clouds that promised rain. Under normal circumstances, he would have been right out there in the middle of everything.

Normal circumstances. He wasn't sure what that meant anymore.

Less than eight hours ago, he had told Shea he wanted her in his bed. How normal was that? For a minute it had been hard to tell which one of them was more shocked. He for saying it. She upon hearing it. In the end, she had simply said she wasn't sure how she felt about him, herself, anything. She might as well have given him a flat "no" right then and there, because he figured that's what she would do eventually. He was willing to bet his next paycheck she would analyze whatever was happening between them until she could justify a reason for running away from it.

And what had been his brilliant response? To tell her he would give her time and respect her space?

Not on your life. He'd kissed her again and told her he wasn't giving up. Told her he intended to pursue her. And she had looked at him as if he'd lost his mind. He probably had.

Reese almost groaned at the memory. He'd never said anything like that to a woman in his life. He'd never had to. But then, he'd never met anyone like Shea. Sharp and sassy one minute, fire in his arms the next. And what fire. Yet each time they kissed, he had sensed a moment of... hesitation? No, more like uncertainty. Almost as if...as if...

No, she couldn't be, could she? Surely not in this day and age. Was it possible Shea had never been with a man before? That would account for her on-and-off, up-and-down behavior where he was concerned. And if that was true, no wonder she had been confused. He hadn't helped the situation any with his proclamation of pursuit. He had kissed her, told her he wanted her...and nothing else. No soft words, no endearments. Just desire.

"No question about it, cowboy. When you screw up, you do it royally."

But was the situation hopeless? God, he hoped not. Somehow, someway, he had to convince her that they could be good for each other. That thought alone was bothersome. He'd never had to convince a woman in his life, and he wondered if that wasn't behind his compelling interest in Shea. Was it just a question of pride? He didn't think so, but it was possible.

And then there was the jealousy thing.

Twice now he'd fought the urge to do bodily harm to a man simply because he had shown an interest in Shea. Luke Tucker had been easy to dismiss, but Dev was something different. Reese had known Devlin O'Brian for years, he was a friend. Yeah, Dev was smooth when it came to the ladies, but he was no sleazebag. Yet Reese had taken one look at the way Dev was smiling and holding Shea's hand, and all he saw was red. If he hadn't practically hauled Shea out of Dev's clutches, he honestly wasn't sure what might have happened.

Oh hell, he knew what would have happened. He would have punched Dev's lights out. Not an admission easily made or accepted.

This whole thing made him crazy. She made him crazy, but he couldn't stop thinking about her, wanting her.

Suddenly Cade's words came back to him with all the accuracy of an arrow hitting its target dead center.

Couldn't stop thinking about her, wanting her.... The more I was with her, the more I wanted to be with her, to take care of her, protect her. Not to mention the fact that I couldn't stand the idea of anyone else touching her.

The words fit him like his favorite pair of jeans. Was he...falling for Shea?

Reese shook his head. It didn't make any sense, but the more he thought about it, the more plausible, even possible it sounded. Cade was right about one thing for sure. Shea Alexander was more woman than he bargained for. More woman than he had a right to hope for.

He turned back to his desk but couldn't keep his mind on work. This thing with Shea had taken over his life. He was behind schedule and couldn't seem to concentrate. Items he had planned to take care of seemed unimportant compared to Shea.

Except one, he thought with a heavy sigh. Natalie.

Natalie, his sweet, agreeable, perfect woman. Brother, when fate decided to turn a man's life around, it sure could be a helluva twist.

Through their correspondence, he'd grown fond of Natalie, and it was only right and fair that he write her one last letter explaining what had happened to him. Shea had happened to him. And even if, God forbid, she didn't love him, Reese knew he could never be happy with Natalie or anyone like her. Sweet was fine, but he had discovered he liked a little spice with his sugar.

Dreading what he had to do, he sat down and began to write a letter to Natalie. Strangely enough, the words flowed easily. But then, he'd felt comfortable sharing with Natalie right from her first letter. Before he knew it, he had poured out his heart to this woman he'd never met, yet felt so close to. Despite the fact that essentially he was writing a Dear Jane letter, he felt Natalie would understand, because she understood loneliness. He hoped she found the man of her dreams. She deserved the very best.

Satisfied he had broken off their correspondence as gently as possible, he sealed the letter and stuck it in his pocket with the intention of driving into town later to mail it.

Now he felt free to find a way to show Shea that he was more than she'd bargained for. More and better.

And the growers association dinner dance that

night was as good a place to start as any. Some good food, pleasant company and music. Add some soft words and maybe he had the right combination for romance.

"I REALLY DON'T THINK it's appropriate for me to go."

"Don't be silly," Belle insisted. "I can't go. And it's a shame to make poor Reese go stag when he could escort a perfectly beautiful woman."

"I'm just not any good at these kinds of social things. I have an idea. Reese and Cade could go as representatives of the winery, and I'll stay home with you."

"Now that *is* silly. First, Cade won't stray more than fifty feet away from me. I don't know which is worse, me being sentenced to bed rest, or having him as my keeper. Second, you told Reese you would go. It's too late to back out now."

Trapped.

That's exactly how she felt. After their ride to the O'Brian ranch, she'd spent the rest of the day trying to avoid being alone with Reese. With limited success. In fact, she would swear he'd been following her, because it seemed every time she turned around, there he was. Now this.

There was no way to gracefully extricate herself from having to be polite and cool to a man who was hot after her body, and in a room full of strangers, no less. Great. Just great, Shea thought.

"What are you going to wear?" Belle asked.

"I haven't the vaguest idea. I don't think I even brought anything suitable."

"Not to worry." Belle laughed. "I've got a closet

full of dressy clothes I can't wear. Most of my long stuff will be too long for you, and you're a bit smaller through the hips, but... Oh, I know. There's a great little blue dress with a bolero jacket that would look stunning on you. It's brand-new. I never had a chance to wear it before I got pregnant. Why don't you go ahead, take a nice, leisurely bath, and when you're done, we'll go upstairs—"

"Over my dead body," Cade said from the doorway. "You, my love, are not setting one foot on those stairs."

Belle looked at Shea and shrugged. "Busted."

"Damn straight."

"If you hadn't protested," Shea told Cade, "I was about to."

"Two against one. I know when I'm licked. Please, help yourself to anything I've got."

"Are you sure? I really don't have to go."

"Sure you do. Reese is looking forward to it," Cade added.

"I wouldn't bet on that," Shea said, resigned to her fate. "All right, I guess I'll go rob your closet."

"And come down for a preview before Reese picks you up, will you?"

"Sure."

Why not? Shea thought as she trudged upstairs. She might as well be dressed to kill. After the tension between her and Reese this morning, the evening was dead in the water before it even started.

She showered, applied some makeup and thought about going to rob Belle's closet, but she just couldn't seem to work up any enthusiasm. All she could think about was spending a whole evening with Reese, knowing he wanted to make love to her.

"Correction. Delete make love. Insert have sex." She put down the brush she'd been using to tame her hair into a french twist and walked to the window to stare at the gathering clouds. Reese had never mentioned the word *love* or confessed to any feelings for her at all. He wanted her in his bed. He wanted sex. And it would probably, undoubtedly be wonderful sex, but nothing more.

"Then what's the problem? For crying out loud, here's your chance to move from correspondence school to postgraduate studies in one giant leap."

And why shouldn't she? After all, it was high time she started living her life instead of dreaming about living it. High time she put her "education" into practice. There was absolutely nothing wrong with enjoying a physical relationship with a man. And Reese appeared to be a willing candidate. They were both consenting adults. Free to do as they pleased.

It was simple. All she had to do was say, "Sure. A quick roll in the hay? Why not?" Nothing to it.

Only there was a lot more to it. Like her feelings for Reese. Like the fact that she had fallen head over heels in love with him.

Well, there it was, the dreaded *L* word. The thing she had feared most and longed for at the same time. Crazy, but there it was, plain as the nose on her face. She was in love with Reese.

Unfortunately for her.

But she wasn't about to wallow in self-pity. She'd seen this coming and done nothing to avoid it. Oh sure, she'd made a couple of protestations and promises to resist what she knew was a one-way trip to heartache, but they were weak and she knew it. No, she didn't have anyone to blame but herself. Reese had made it clear: he wanted to take her to bed. Not to the altar.

Not that she expected him to pledge his undying love. She wasn't that naive. But it would be nice to have a couple of sweet nothings whispered in her ear first.

First?

It sounded as if she had made the decision to go to bed with him.

"If it walks like a duck," she said, a little disgusted for not debating the issue with herself as she usually did. No pros or cons this time, no rebuttals. No siree, just go with the flow. Actually, go with her feelings. For the first time in her life she was deliberately avoiding a thorough analysis of the situation. Deliberately avoiding any and all valid reasons why she shouldn't jump into Reese's bed. Logic would mess up everything in a heartbeat.

Besides, she would have plenty of time for logic later. Once she was back in Austin, away from Reese, she would have all the time in the world to…reflect? Regret? Probably. Maybe. Truthfully, she expected making love with Reese would break her heart. Given that certainty, it did seem that her decision was the act of a fool. But she had also decided that perhaps fools had an advantage over the rest of the world. They blundered through life, taking joy where they found it. How foolhardy was that? For someone whose entire life and all of her self-worth were based on a framework of facts, it sounded like freedom.

Tonight there'd be fireworks and bells, emancipation and graduation all rolled into one. Even if tonight was all she would ever have? She hoped and prayed it wasn't, but if that was the case, there would still be no regrets. For as long as it lasted.

She was going to grab for the brass ring. For once in her life, she was going to be an ordinary woman in love.

BELLE'S GREAT LITTLE blue dress turned out to be totally unlike anything Shea had ever worn before in her life. It definitely wasn't long. In fact, the hem barely came to the middle of her thighs, and as for fit... The blend of silk and Lycra fabric, a little shimmery, a lot sexy, clung to her body like a second skin. And what wasn't covered by clinging fabric was left bare. Like her arms and back. And the fact that she was slightly more endowed than Belle had ever been was more apparent in this dress...particularly since she couldn't wear a bra. Shea had taken one look at herself in the mirror and panicked. She couldn't wear something so...so blatant, even if she did intend to sleep with Reese. One thumb of her nose at convention was enough. So she had pulled out her best suit, changed and gone downstairs. Belle had immediately nixed the suit as too businesslike, not appropriate, and sent her back to the little blue dress.

"Thank God for this," Shea murmured as she tugged the long-sleeved bolero jacket, made of the same fabric and piped in black silk, over her breasts. The edges didn't quite meet, but that was all right because she didn't plan on taking it off all night. She scooped up a small black bag, also borrowed, from the bed and headed downstairs for the second time.

Cade was standing in the foyer sorting through a stack of mail when he heard her on the stairs. He glanced up...and his mouth dropped open. "Holy cow."

Shea stopped. "It's too short, isn't it? I should change, shouldn't I?"

"Only if you don't want to give half the men at the party tonight a heart attack." He gave a long, low whistle of appreciation. "You're gonna make men stutter and women green with envy."

"Really?" She was accustomed to compliments on her intellect and her business acumen, but not her looks. "Then it looks okay? You think Reese will like it?"

He grinned. "Trust me, Shea. He'll love it."

The doorbell rang and Shea's heart began to race.

"You're gonna knock his socks off," Cade assured her as he left her to her fate.

She crossed her fingers then walked over to open the door.

Holding a florist box behind his back, Reese swept his hat off. "Good..." His eyes widened. "God almighty."

"Good evening, Reese," she said, thrilled by his reaction. "I'm ready to go." She gave in to a whim and glanced at his feet. If his socks had been knocked off, she couldn't tell. He was wearing boots.

"Uh? What?" He was staring, but who

wouldn't. That dress was…and those legs… How come he'd never noticed how long and shapely her legs were before? They were incredible, especially in those sheer black hose. But that dress…

"I said I'm ready to go."

"Oh, uh…" Suddenly he remembered the flowers. "Here. I almost forgot…I mean, these are for you." He thrust the box at her.

She stared at the box containing a corsage of three perfect gardenias. "For me?"

The shock of seeing her in that dress was beginning to wear off. "Of course."

No one had ever brought her flowers, and for a moment, Shea thought she might cry. In fact, her eyes misted slightly. She looked at Reese. "Thank you. They're…they're lovely."

"Want me to put them on you?"

"No, I'll just pin them to my purse."

He settled his hat on his head and offered her his arm, and they stepped out into the night.

"You think we'll need an umbrella?" she asked, gazing at the threatening sky.

"Haven't heard a rumble of thunder or seen a flicker of lightning," he said as they went down the front steps toward his truck. "Hope you don't mind going in my truck. I tried to spiff it up some, but—"

"I don't mind." The truck was as clean and shiny as if it had just rolled off the showroom floor.

Reese opened the door and took her hand to help her inside. "Oh," she said, unable to gracefully climb into the truck without her hemline creeping up several more inches. "Would you hold this?" She held out her bag. As soon as Shea handed it over, she put her palms behind her on the seat, the heel of her shoe on the running board, and tried to scoot up and back into the truck. It didn't work, so she tried again.

It was a good thing she was so focused on getting into the truck or she would have seen Reese's tongue hanging out. Every move she made caused the dress to ride up her thigh and his blood pressure to climb. Finally, he couldn't take any more. "Here." He tossed her purse onto the seat, put his hands on her waist and lifted her into the truck.

She swung her legs inside, tugging her dress down. "Thank you."

"No problem." He closed the door, walked slowly around to the driver's side. The whole time he was telling himself to get a grip on his hormones before he embarrassed both of them. Thank goodness the drive into Lubbock would give him a few minutes to cool down.

Reese said very little as they drove into the city. He was quiet and distant. There was none of the intensity he'd shown that morning when he told her he wanted her. The only thing Shea could figure out was that he had changed his mind. After several more minutes of almost frosty silence, she couldn't stand it.

"Where is the dinner being held?" she asked as they neared the university.

"One of the members' fathers is J. D. Hyatt, and—"

"The oil tycoon?"

"Yeah. The Hyatts offered to host the event."

"They must have a huge home."

"It covers a few acres."

A few acres? Shea thought, once they arrived and Reese handed his keys to the valet. A few hundred was more like it. The house was three stories and covered at least an acre by itself. They walked up multiple sets of exquisitely landscaped terraced stairways that worked their way around one end of the house. The steps led to four tennis courts, two of which were tented to host the event.

The tented area could accommodate approximately one hundred people and included a dance floor and bandstand. As they walked in, several men noticed their entrance and came over to greet Reese. It was obvious he was well liked and respected among the growers. In fact, so many people came over to say hello that Shea was pushed to the background. She started to protest, then changed her mind. She had been so preoccupied with her own appearance that she had taken little time to appreciate his. Now, standing back, she had an excellent opportunity to admire him. And admire him she did, telling herself her appraisal was objective, when all along she knew it was a lie. How could she be objective where Reese was concerned?

The black Western-cut suit he wore was beautifully tailored and better looking than any tuxedo. Undoubtedly custom-made, she decided. It had to be to fit those shoulders. His shirt looked stark white against his tan skin and black hair. The black-and-white combination might have appeared severe had it not been for the turquoise and onyx bolo tie set in silver. Matching cuff links winked in the light of the crystal chandelier above him as he reached to shake a newcomer's hand.

Strange, she thought. He stood among the men, yet he didn't seem to be a part of the group. It was almost as if he stood on the fringe, content to have a tentative connection but not join in. Maybe that's what made him seem at least a head taller than the men around him. Or maybe that was because in her mind, he dominated whatever space he occupied. A domination that had little to do with stature, although he was no slouch in that department. In fact, from where she stood, Reese Barrett looked to be about as close to perfect as a man could get.

And just for tonight, she sighed wistfully, she could pretend he was hers.

As if he'd heard her sigh, Reese turned his head. Their gazes locked, and for a few seconds, Shea forgot to breathe. How could any man be that gorgeous? She stared, almost spellbound, as he separated himself from the men and came toward her.

"Sorry. Did you think I'd forgotten you?"

"No. Don't apologize. I know there's always a certain amount of schmoozing that goes on at an affair like this."

"They're just shootin' the bull."

"I don't want to take you away if—"

"And leave a beautiful woman by herself?" He took her hand and tucked it in his arm. "Not on your life. Every man in this room has got to be jealous of me tonight."

Shea didn't know what to say to such a dazzling compliment. Especially after his silence on the drive there. Relieved, she smiled and let him lead her to the table they would share with three other couples. There was a short before-dinner speech from the president of the association, then the meal was served. The conversation was polite and the food tasty, but Shea had a hard time concentrating on either with Reese sitting beside her. Several times during the meal, he leaned close to ask if her steak was cooked right, or did she want more tea or coffee.

And each time he managed to touch her.

A brush of his hand against hers. Accidental shoulder-to-shoulder contact. Outwardly insignificant, but they made her blood heat and her heart race. Each touch was like an electric shock sizzling along her nerve endings. She found herself anticipating the next time, waiting for that sensual thrill. It got to the point that she wished it had been just the two of them in some small restaurant instead of a crowded banquet hall.

And then, she got her wish, sort of.

Dessert and coffee cleared away, Reese stood and held out his hand. "Would you like to dance?"

Her experience on the dance floor was only marginally better than her experience with men, but she would never capture the brass ring if she didn't reach. She took a deep breath and put her hand in his. "Just promise you'll catch me if I stumble."

"No problem. You'll be in my arms the whole time."

It was heaven.

She rested her head on his chest and savored the moment. Until the music ended, she could stay in the shelter of his strong arms and pretend that it could be forever. She'd once thought she was no good at pretending, but tonight she *wanted* to pretend. So much so, that she hated for the music to end. Worse, after one dance Reese was ready to leave. But the evening was still so young! Now she realized he'd given the compliment lightly. He wasn't treating her like a women he desired. He must have changed his mind.

Reese knew he had peeled out of the Hyatt estate parking lot like a bat out of hell. If he didn't slow down, he'd likely get a ticket. Perfect, he thought. Maybe they would throw him in jail. At least that way he would be beyond temptation.

The temptation sitting next to him.

What happened to his good intentions? He was going to whisper sweet words in her ear and court her. All he had done all night was fight the urge to haul her out of that dinner and straight to the nearest motel. He'd tried to blame the dress, but it wasn't the dress. It was the woman in it. Actually there was no one to blame but himself. God, but she had him tied in knots. As they drove, the first rumbles of thunder rolled through the night, followed by the distant crackle of lightning.

"I, uh, had a nice time," Shea said, breaking the silence.

"Good."

"All of the people I met seemed very nice."

"Yeah, they all thought you were…nice, too."

"That's—" she almost said nice "—wonderful."

The truth was, she had charmed everyone at their table. And he'd spent half his time sending killer looks at all of the unmarried men ogling her and a couple of the married ones, too. He couldn't stand the thought that one of them might cut in, so after one measly dance, he had all but dragged her home.

When they turned into the driveway to the ranch house, Shea realized he was ready to end the evening. Desperation clutched at her heart. She had to do something, say something, or she would never have this night with him. Maybe her only night. And if she wasn't going to get her chance, then dammit, she deserved to know why he had changed his mind.

"I'd like to go to your cabin," she blurted out.

Reese hit the brakes. "What?"

She summoned all her courage. "Well, it's still early, and I thought maybe we could have some coffee and...talk."

"Talk?" The last thing he wanted to do with her was talk. "About what?"

"Things."

He looked at her, the road, then back at her. Without another word he drove on past the main house to his cabin. He parked in front and escorted her inside. Shea walked to the sofa and sat down. Reese stayed by the front door staring, just staring. Seconds of silence stretched for what seemed like hours, the only sound a gentle patter as rain began to fall against the windows. Finally, they both decided to break the silence at once.

"Shea—"

"Reese—"

"You go first," he offered.

"Well...well, it's just that this morning you said you wanted...wanted me in..."

"I know what I said."

"Yes. And, uh, I realize...that is, I..."

Reese ran a hand through his hair. "Look, Shea—"

"No, wait. Let me say this. It's obvious to me that you've changed your mind—"

"Changed your mind?"

"And, of course, you have that right. I'm not faulting you. It's just that—"

"Changed my mind?"

"I'd really like to know why. There, I'm done," she said, running out of breath and nerve at the same time.

Reese couldn't believe it. She actually thought he had stopped wanting her? How could she possibly...? Then he remembered his earlier suspicion that she might be a virgin. This would take delicate handling, he decided. Slowly, in order to give himself time to back down from the need hammering in his body, he took off his coat, removed the bolo tie, undid three buttons on his shirt and rolled his sleeves to midforearm. Then he started toward the kitchen.

Shea glanced over her shoulder. "Where are you going?"

"Thought you wanted coffee and conversation."

"I've...no, I don't want any coffee." Lord knew her nerves were bad enough without caffeine.

Reese walked to the end of the sofa but no closer. He didn't trust himself to get any closer.

"Why...why don't you sit down and we'll—"

He shook his head. "No. Not right now." She looked down at her hands folded in her lap, but not before he saw disappointment in her eyes and realized she had taken his answer as a rejection. "Shea."

She looked up. "Yes."

"Why would you think I've changed my mind about wanting you in my bed?"

"Why?" Either the man had a colossal ego or he enjoyed seeing her squirm. Pride suffused her frayed nerves with enough strength to take what bits of dignity she still possessed and get out as quickly as possible.

"To begin with, you hardly spoke on the way to dinner. We danced once, then you promptly hauled me off the dance floor and hustled me into your truck. When we got home, you couldn't wait to dump me at the front door. Now you don't even want to sit next to me." Frustrated, she stood up. "And now that I have made a complete fool out of myself, I'm leaving."

He cut off her escape route. "You're not going anywhere until I tell you a thing or two."

"I'm no longer interested," she lied.

He ignored her comment. "I didn't say much because my tongue was practically hanging out of my mouth. I took one look at you in that dress you've got on and I wasn't sure I could keep from eating you alive. How short is that damned thing, anyway? Never mind. I don't wanna know."

Now it was Shea's turn to stare. She couldn't believe what she was hearing.

"As for hauling you off the dance floor, I couldn't have lived through another minute of having you in my arms and not kissing you. As for dumping you at the front door—let's just say I was able to overcome my baser instincts. Anything else? Oh, yes. Sitting. Well, it was either stand here and try to act like a gentleman, or sit beside you and rip your clothes off." He took a deep breath. "I think that answers all of your objections."

"It certainly does," she whispered, a sweet satisfaction growing inside her. He still wanted her. "So you still—"

"Yeah. I do."

She reached out to him. "Reese—"

"Just..." He held up a hand and wasn't surprised to notice it was trembling. "Just a minute. I need to ask you something. Something...personal."

"All right."

"And I don't want you to get riled."

"I won't."

"Wouldn't be too sure."

"Just ask me, Reese."

"Okay. Are you... I got the impression you've never... What I mean is, have you ever been with a man before?"

Shea blinked, totally surprised by his question. "What difference does that make?"

"A helluva lot to me. I'm not in the habit of taking— Well, I just don't, that's all."

"You want to know if I'm a virgin."

"Yes."

"No." But before he could breathe a sigh of relief, she added, "Not...technically, anyway."

"What does that mean?"

"Do we have to talk about it?"

Instantly, he was concerned. "You weren't

abused, were you?'' He closed his eyes, doubled his fists. "God, please tell me—"

"No. I wasn't. "

He opened his eyes. "Then—"

"It was only once, and it wasn't very good. I didn't even…"

Relief flooded his body. "You trying to tell me the earth didn't move?"

"I'm trying to tell you *I* barely moved before it was over."

Reese glanced down, partly to hide a smile. This was not a laughing matter, but he'd be worse than a hypocrite if he didn't admit to feeling pleased that no other man had ever pleasured her. Still, she was treading unfamiliar ground, and he cautioned himself to take it easy, let her adjust to passion at her own pace. When he lifted his gaze to hers, his eyes were soft, compelling. "Come here."

When she came to him without hesitation, he touched her cheek. "I can't promise you the earth will move. But I can promise you two things."

"What?'' She opened her eyes.

"I'll make certain you get the chance to move. And it'll be better than good." He kissed her then, slowly, gently, his lips verifying the promise he'd just made as he took her in his arms. At least the kiss started out that way. Before too long their bodies ignited fires neither wanted to control.

Shea wound her arms around his neck as a now familiar and welcome heat sizzled through her body, leaving in its wake a hunger for more. Moving closer, she moaned as his tongue touched hers. "Reese," she murmured.

"Oh, Bright Eyes, you taste so good." He tightened his hold on her. "Feel so good." When he fastened his mouth on hers again, the kiss was urgent, needy. Her response was the same.

"Take off this jacket," he said, tugging at it even as he spoke.

"Yes. Just—" She sighed as he kissed her neck "—wait until I…" Shea struggled to unhook the buttons at the wrists. "There," she said as he peeled it from her shoulders, leaving her arms and back bare.

"If I had known there was nothing but you under that jacket when we were dancing, there's no telling what I might have done."

In all the maneuvering to remove the jacket, they had worked their way to the sofa. Before she knew it, he sat down, pulling her into his lap. "I want you to kiss me, Shea. You set the pace. Do you understand?"

"I—I think so."

"Then kiss me. Touch me. I'm dying to have your hands on me."

Shea leaned forward and kissed him lightly, then pulled back to look into his eyes. "Aren't you going to kiss me back?"

Reese clamped down on his need. "In time. For now, I want you to enjoy exploring. Just do what feels good." He grinned. "Trust me. There's nothing you can do that I won't enjoy, too."

Trust me, he'd asked. Even though there'd been no words of love exchanged, she spoke them in her heart. Trust him? Oh, yes. With her body and her heart. She smiled and leaned forward again, only this time she rubbed her mouth back and forth across his, savoring the warmth, the texture of his lips. Once, twice, and then she realized she was teasing herself as much as him. Then her hands were in his hair, holding him for her kiss. A real kiss, deep with longing, hot with need.

"You're learning fast," he said when she broke contact long enough to slide deeper into his lap. Full breasts flattened against the hard wall of his chest.

"Am I?"

"Yeah." Of course, at this rate he wasn't sure if he'd live to see graduation.

"Can I unbutton your shirt?"

"Help yourself."

She did, spreading the front so her hands could glide across his chest. "You have a gorgeous body. I like the way your skin feels." Lowering her head, she kissed his throat.

Reese moaned.

"Do...do you want to touch me?" she asked breathlessly.

"I ache to touch you."

She sighed, feeling treasured. Slowly, she raised a hand to push the strap of her dress from one shoulder, and with a tug of her finger, she pulled the front low enough to expose the swell of her breasts. "Please," she whispered.

Reese pushed the shimmering material the rest of the way down. At the sight of her perfect breasts, he almost forgot to breathe. *Stunning* was the first word that came to mind. He reached out a fingertip and stroked one, then the other.

Shea gasped, then sighed, her hand clutching at his shirtfront. "That feels so..." A shiver of need went through her body. Her nipples tightened, ached. A strange cross between pleasure and pain. "So good."

"It gets better." He leaned forward, gently kissing a soft swell. Then slowly, he drew a line of kisses from her breast to her neck and back again. This time he didn't stop until he closed his mouth over her nipple.

"Reese," she whispered as ripples of exquisite sensations radiated from his lips through her whole body, making it hum. Making it buzz with need. "Reese…"

For a moment Reese thought the sound he heard was Shea moaning, then he realized it wasn't coming from her. It was coming from two sources. Their pagers, his in his pocket, hers in her purse.

He dragged his mouth away, leaving her damp and breathing hard.

"Damn!"

"Wh-what is it?"

"Damn," he said again, easing her from his lap onto the sofa. "It's my pager." He reached into his pocket.

Shea had forgotten Cade had given both of them pagers in case he was out on the ranch when Belle went into labor. She sat up straight. "Belle!"

Reese held the pager so she could see the readout. One word, but it was enough.

Baby!

9

"THANK GOD YOU'RE HERE," Cade said as Reese and Shea raced into the converted study. He was holding Belle's hand while she moaned, in the middle of a contraction.

"Is this it?" Reese asked.

"Yeah. Paramedics—that's it, darlin', breathe, breathe—should be here—breathe, breathe. Stay focused." He gestured toward her focal point, a framed photo of Caesar Farentino on the table beside the bed. "Any minute."

"What about her obstetrician?"

"Called him."

Reese and Shea had scrambled off his sofa and made a mad dash though the driving rain to the house. Now, standing there in Reese's wet jacket, Shea bit her lip in sympathy for the pain etched on her friend's face. The sound of Belle's panting filled the room.

Shea felt Reese move to stand close behind her. He put a hand on her shoulder and squeezed. Grateful for his strength, she leaned against him. "Can we do anything?" she asked.

Cade shook his head, but she caught the worried glance he sent Reese. They all knew the baby was coming too early.

The contraction subsided and Belle relaxed

while Cade bathed her face with a cool cloth. "Hi," she said, managing a weak smile. "Glad you guys...are here."

"Wouldn't be anywhere else," Reese assured her.

"How...was the...party?"

"Fine." Shea smiled, trying to match Belle's courage. She couldn't imagine what it was like to know the child you were carrying was coming into the world too soon and might face Lord knew what medical difficulties. *Please, God. Don't let anything happen to either of them.*

"Must be...raining." Belle reached for Cade's hand again.

"A real gully-washer," Reese told her. "No tellin'—"

Belle's gasp cut him off as another contraction tightened her body, and at the same time they heard a siren. Seconds later two paramedics clambered through the front door and across the tiled foyer, bringing a gurney with them.

Even though Shea had witnessed this scene before, some instinct told her this time was different. For real. Belle's baby was about to be born.

In a matter of minutes Belle was on the gurney and headed out the door, with Cade following.

"Get come dry clothes. We can change at the hospital," Reese told Shea. "I'll pick you up in five minutes."

THEY HAD BOTH CHANGED clothes as soon as they were assured Belle was indeed in labor and there was nothing they could do but wait. Reese now wore faded jeans, a Western-cut shirt and what he called his everyday boots. Shea, too, wore jeans and a long-sleeved shirt, but in her haste to meet him, she had snagged her sneakers but no socks. Her feet were cold in the almost frigid waiting room. The storm, still raging with high winds and pelting rain, had lowered the outside temperature, but the hospital thermostat hadn't been adjusted. She wished they had some news. The waiting was torture.

"I wish to hell someone would come out and let us know what's going on." Reese paced in front of the chair where Shea sat. "It's been almost three hours."

"The waiting's hard." She had tried for the last hour to read an article in an outdated copy of *People* magazine, but it was no use. She pitched the magazine onto the table at her right and watched him pace. "Remember, they had to do a C-section," she reminded him. "That's surgery."

"I know. And I don't like it. What if something went wrong? What if—"

"Don't! You'll just make yourself...and me...crazy with questions like that." She shot out of the chair and walked to the window, then back to where he stood. "We have to believe everything will be all right, you hear me? It's very important. As soon as she's taken to recovery, Cade will find us."

"I'm sorry." Reese took both her hands in his. "This is as hard on you as it is on me. I know how much you care about Belle."

"No more than you do."

He put his arms around her and a smile tilted one corner of his mouth. "You know, if it wasn't for the fact that we're about to welcome a new McBride into the world, I'd say this was lousy timing."

Shea glanced up, smiling. "Just think how lousy it would have been fifteen minutes later."

"Oh, no. Fate wouldn't be that cruel." He hugged her to him and felt her shiver. "Are you cold?"

"I was before you put your arms around me. Now you make me shiver."

His gaze went to her mouth. "Me, too. I want to kiss you."

Just that quick, the air in the waiting room thickened to the consistency of molasses and Shea's heart shifted into high gear. They were in a public place, yet she felt every bit as intimate as when they had been in his cabin. She suddenly realized that true intimacy had nothing to do with sex and everything to do with a feeling of rightness or belonging. She'd known it intellectually but had never understood what it meant. And if she hadn't known she was in love with Reese before, she knew it now. Nothing in her life had ever felt as good, as right.

"We shouldn't...should we?"

"Probably no—" But his mouth was on hers before he finished the sentence.

Shea thought she might just suffocate, but a lungful of air wasn't worth the loss of his kiss. The heat speared through her body, streaking along her nerve endings, sizzling in her blood.

His hands moved over her narrow back, then up her sides until the heels of his hands pressed against the side of her breasts. He needed to touch them, ached to possess them. Frustration twisted inside him. He was almost past the point of caring where they were, when—

"Hey!"

They broke apart, both turning to see who had interrupted them. Cade was standing at the entrance to the waiting room wearing a Texas-size grin.

"It's a boy! I've got a son."

Shea and Reese moved at the same time. She raced over, threw her arms around Cade's neck and kissed him. Reese raced over and pumped his hand.

"How's Belle?"

"Is everything all right?"

"What did you name him? How much does he weigh?"

"Whoa." Cade held up his hands. "Slow down, you two. Belle's fine. Chance is—"

"Chance?" Reese grinned.

Cade grinned back. "Yeah. Guess you were right. It's not a bad name for a kid." When Shea looked puzzled, he explained. "Reese once told me a kid of Belle's and mine didn't stand a chance of being anything but hardheaded with us as parents."

"It's a great name," Shea gushed. "How much does he weigh?"

A tiny bit of the glow faded from Cade's smile. "Not as much as they would like, but he's doin' great. He'll probably have to stay in the hospital for a week to ten days, but the doc says his lungs look really good, and that's what they want in a preemie."

"A preemie?"

"It's what they call premature babies." At Reese's frown, Cade hurried to reassure him. "He really is fine. I quizzed the doctor up one side and down the other." Cade scrubbed his face with both hands. "I'm not sure, but I think I threatened him if he didn't tell me the truth."

Reese grinned. "Then we can probably take whatever he says to the bank."

"Can we see Belle?" Shea asked.

He shook his head. "They gave her something. She's zonked. But the doc said it would be okay to visit tomorrow." The Texas-size grin reappeared. "You can see Chance."

It was all Shea could do to keep from jumping up and down. "Now?"

"Right now."

The three of them walked down the hall to the nursery, and Shea and Reese were introduced to Robert Chance McBride. "We decided on Robert," Cade said, "because Caesar's first name was Roberto."

The dark-haired infant was in an incubator, and at first sight of him, Shea gasped. "Cade!" She clutched at his sleeve.

"Sorry, I should have prepared you. But it looks a lot worse than it is. They've got him hooked up to monitors and stuff to check his heart rate and body temperature. The good news is he's breathing on his own with no respiratory problems whatsoever."

Reese stood next to Shea. "I gotta say you're taking this a whole lot calmer than I would, Ace."

"I'd probably be a basket case if I hadn't done

some reading on premature deliveries. Right now, Chance weighs almost five pounds. That makes him a heavyweight in the world of preemies.''

''Well, he's got McBride and Farentino blood in his veins, so he's bound to be a scrapper.''

''Damn straight.''

For several long minutes, the three stood and simply enjoyed watching young Robert Chance in his first hour of life. Shea looked at the baby, fascinated by this little miracle and fearful at the same time. Like Cade, she had been reading up on babies. Not to the extent he had, but enough to know this baby faced a battle. Such tiny fingers, such a narrow little chest, she thought, straining to watch its almost imperceptible rise and fall. She had never been around a baby, never even realized she longed to be. Now she did. Watching Chance, she was overwhelmed by a feeling of connection to this tiny newborn. He was part of someone she loved, and already she loved him. But despite every assurance Cade had given them, she was still afraid for the child. He was so small, so helpless, and there were so many things that could go wrong. She couldn't take her eyes off him.

Finally, with a deep sigh, Cade turned to Reese. ''I gotta get back to Belle. I wanna be there when she wakes up. Is it still raining?''

''Buckets,'' Reese said.

''Well then, you guys better get your butts home. One of the nurses told me there was some flash flooding.''

''Sure you don't want us to stay?''

''Nothing you can do. I'd appreciate it if you'd

make sure everything is tied down and closed up when you get back to the ranch?"

"You know I will."

"Yeah. And check on Dolly, will you? I just hope she hasn't taken it into her head to bust out again."

"Maybe Tyler gave her a tranquilizer when he saw the clouds."

"Hope so." Cade turned to Shea. "Thanks for being here. It meant a lot to Belle."

"I wouldn't have been anywhere else."

"And don't worry about a thing. Shea and I will make sure everything is safe and sound," Reese assured him.

When Cade was well out of earshot, Shea turned to Reese. "He's so little," she whispered, as if saying it any louder might suddenly make the baby smaller.

"I know." He had seen Cade in a lot of different situations over the years, some dicey and a few downright dangerous. But in all their years of friendship, he had never seen Cade try to bullshit him. Until tonight. Cade McBride was worried. Reese accepted that at least some of what Cade had told them was true, but he had a feeling he'd also left out some things. Like survival statistics on preemies. "I keep thinking, what if—"

Shea whipped around to face him and there were tears in her eyes. "No what-ifs. This baby is going to make it. No more negative thoughts from either of us. Okay?"

Reese touched her cheek. "Whatever you say, Bright Eyes."

IT TOOK THEM almost an hour to get home. More than once Reese had to slow down to a crawl in order to navigate some high-water areas.

Peering into the darkness, Shea said, "I didn't think this part of Texas got this much rain."

"Usually it doesn't. But every so often, we seem to get it all at once."

They made it home, mainly because Reese's truck cleared the road enough to thwart the mud. And there was a lot of mud. Several times the truck slid sideways on the muddy road, barely missing a bar ditch. Shea breathed a sigh of relief when they pulled into the driveway of the ranch.

"You mind hanging around while I batten down the hatches?" he asked.

"No. Not at all."

Reese drove straight to the barn, parked, then reached under the front seat and pulled out a plastic rain poncho. "I'll only be a minute."

"Got another one of those? I'll go with you."

"No, but there's plenty of room under here."

Shea smiled. "Okay."

They scurried into the barn, arms around each other's waists, the poncho over their heads and torsos. As soon as they were out of the rain, Reese tossed the poncho over the door of a stall.

He shook the water from his hair then walked over to an open stall. "Well." He put his hands on his hips. "At least this time she only busted the latch and not the whole damn door."

"Are all the other horses still here?"

"Yeah. Looks like Tyler has done a good job of locking up. He probably just missed Dolly. I'd better check in with him."

Before Reese could turn around, a phone mounted on a wall at the end of a row of stalls started ringing. He jogged to the phone and snatched up the receiver. After a short conversation he walked back to her.

"It's just as I figured. Tyler came in to make sure Dolly was okay and she was gone."

"What happens now?"

"I go after her."

"But...forgive me for asking a stupid question—won't she be all right? Don't you have horses out on the open range in this weather?"

"Of course, but you're trying to apply logic to a terrified animal. She just runs, and she has hurt herself in the past. The truth is, we'd let her run, but none of us wants to have to face Belle with the news that her favorite horse is either dead or gone for good. Besides, I have a good idea where she is."

"Where?"

"The last two times she's bolted, Cade and I found her in a wash that ran right past a stand of mesquite trees. It was raining like it would never quit, and she was stuck in the mud."

"And she just comes back with you?"

"Once we got a rope on her, she didn't give us much trouble, although I gotta admit, it worked better with two of us."

"Why not take one of the hands with you?"

"It's late. No sense dragging 'em out in this if I don't have to. C'mon, I'll walk you up to the house."

"Don't worry about me. Do what you need to do. I'll stay until you leave."

"Okay." He took her hand and together they walked to Skedaddle's stall.

Reese left her there while he stepped into the tack room to get his gear. While Shea watched, he quickly saddled the horse, then put on a slicker and slipped a plastic covering over his hat.

"You must have done this a thousand times," she said. "There wasn't one wasted motion."

Reese grinned. "Enough that if I had a nickel for every time, I wouldn't need to work for a living."

He backed the horse out of the stall and into the wide pass through the stables just as a wicked bolt of lightning slashed across the sky. Skedaddle snorted and gave a nervous whinny. Shea knew exactly how the horse felt. Suddenly, the thought of Reese riding out into the storm made her incredibly nervous. She knew he was an expert horseman and experienced in these kinds of animal rescues, but fear gnawed at her. The thought that something might happen to him sent shivers down her spine.

"Reese, I…I…"

"What is it, Bright Eyes?" Ready to ride, he stepped up into the saddle and hung a lantern from his saddle horn.

She wanted to tell him not to go but knew it was just her anxiety. And he probably wouldn't appreciate it one bit if she begged him to take a ranch hand along. "Just…be careful, please."

"For you, darlin', anything." He settled his hat firmly on his head. "You take the poncho and head for the house. I'll call you first thing in the morning."

"No! Call me when you get back."

He looked down at her for a moment then nodded, kicked Skedaddle's flank and rode out into the night.

Shea ran to the stable door in time to see horse and rider pelted by the relentless rain, then swallowed by the night. She had no idea how long she stood there, staring at the spot where he'd disappeared, or when the idea of following him first popped into her head. But the feeling that he needed her, that she had to go after him was overpowering.

"Crazy," she whispered. "You don't know where he went." No, she didn't, but she'd bet Tyler knew the place Reese had described. Shea spun on her heel and ran to the same phone he had used earlier. She didn't care if what she was doing made Reese mad, wounded his pride or any other damned thing. Call it a hunch, but something told her he shouldn't be out there alone and she wasn't going to ignore it. She scanned the list of extensions, found the one for the bunkhouse and punched it in. When she hung up three minutes later, Tyler was on his way.

THE PONCHO HAD KEPT her dry for about ten minutes after they rode away from the barn. Now Shea was soaked from the hips down, her tennis shoes were practically falling off her feet, they held so much water, and she didn't have the vaguest idea where she was. Thank goodness Tyler knew where they were going.

"Should be just over that rise," he shouted, trying to be heard over the downpour.

Shea nodded. Sure enough, they topped the rise

just as fingers of lightning spread across the darkness, illuminating a stand of mesquite trees…and Reese, in the wash, up to his thighs in mud and water.

Clutching a rope around Dolly's neck, with the other end connected to his horse and saddle, he looked up as Tyler and Shea galloped to the edge of the wash. He waved them off. "The bank is a mud slide," he yelled. "Stay back."

Tyler dismounted, taking his rope with him. With only the light from the lantern hanging in one of the trees to help him see, he swung a wide loop over his head for several passes, then threw it to Reese, who worked it over his head and down to his waist. Tyler hooked the other end to his saddle horn and backed his horse up, pulling Reese free. As soon as he loosened the rope and stepped out of it, Reese turned to Shea. "What the hell are you doing out here?"

"She told me you needed help," Tyler said. "You okay?"

Reese nodded, but she could tell he wasn't thrilled to see her.

"What about Dolly?" Tyler asked.

"Stuck. We're gonna need the Jeep," Reese told him. He pointed to Shea. "Go with him."

She shook her head.

"Dammit, Shea. This is no place for you. Go back with Tyler and wait for me."

"No."

If he'd had the time, Reese would have yanked her off that horse and insisted she go home, but he didn't have time. Flash flooding had turned the narrow wash into a river of swirling water and mud. Dolly was in it almost up to her flank and was struggling, wild-eyed with fear.

"Leave the rope and go," he yelled at Tyler. Without further instructions, the ranch hand mounted his horse and took off, leaving Shea to face Reese.

When she started to dismount, he stomped over to her. "Stay in the saddle. Too muddy. Fall and you'll slide right into the water."

One look at the river of murky water rushing so fast it had exposed the roots of the trees was enough to convince her he was right. "What are you doing?" she asked, seeing him struggling with the wet rope.

"Making a rope halter."

Before she could ask another question he turned, heading back to Dolly. She started to call out to him but thought better of it. *He knows what he's doing*, she told herself. *He'll be all right*. But that didn't do much to alleviate her fears, particularly when the next second she watched Reese grab a tree limb and swing himself back into the water. Her heart shot into her throat and she had to put her hand over her mouth to keep from screaming his name.

Reese wedged himself between the roots of two trees closest to Dolly and worked to get the makeshift halter over the terrified horse's head. It seemed that he struggled for an hour with the animal and the elements until finally he had the halter in place. Shea breathed a sigh of relief when she saw him secure the rope to the largest tree, then start to climb out of the water. Relief was premature. The next second he lost his hold on the limb and fell backward into the rushing torrent.

Shea screamed, threw herself out of the saddle and ran toward the water. "Reese! Reese!"

His head broke the surface and at the same time his hand reached out and grabbed a handful of exposed roots. "Get the—" He went under again.

"Reese!" *Oh, God,* she prayed. *Please help him!*

He came up again, sputtering and shaking his head. "Rope. Get your rope."

Shea ran back to her horse to get the rope, then remembered how Tyler had pulled Reese out the first time. After making sure one end of the rope was tied to the saddle horn, she ran back to Reese.

"Throw it," he yelled as he tried to stand up in the fast-moving water.

She did, and it was only in answer to her prayer that he caught it. Shea knew what to do next, and she ran to the horse and climbed into the saddle. "Back," she commanded, pulling on the reins, hollering at the horse to back up until she could see Reese lying on the solid ground beside the wash. "Whoa!" she yelled, almost falling off the horse in her rush to get to him.

"Reese! Are you all right?" On her knees beside him in the mud, she grabbed at his slicker. "Reese!"

He lifted his head and looked at her. "Shea?"

He was covered in mud. His hair was plastered to his head, and he had never looked more handsome. "Oh, God." She threw her arms around his neck. "Thank you, thank you, thank—"

The sound of an engine penetrated the rain, and

suddenly two spots of light were coming toward them. "Tyler," Reese said.

A few moments later the Jeep screeched to a halt and Tyler walked out of the darkness. To Shea, he looked like an angel.

He helped get Reese to his feet, and the two of them, working with ropes and a winch for another half hour, rescued the beleaguered horse. Finally, the equally wet and muddy humans and horses were all on solid, safe ground.

"You can drive the Jeep back," Reese told Shea. "I'll ride."

"You're drenched."

"So are you. What's a few more drops of water."

"Damned if I'm gonna stand here and argue with you. Let's get dry."

He helped her mount up and they headed for home while Tyler followed slowly with Dolly in tow. The Jeep rolled right into the barn and stopped. Reese dismounted and helped Shea down.

"I've got it under control," Tyler said. "Why don't you two get into some dry clothes."

"Good idea." Reese took Shea by the hand, and together they walked back out into the rain.

Halfway to the main house, Shea stopped him. "I can't go into the house like this."

Reese looked at her. The hood to the poncho had long since slipped off and her hair hung in wet strands around her face and neck. She had fallen in the mud so many times that she, too, was covered with a good portion of the Panhandle. And her poor feet...were bare.

"Where are your shoes?"

She pointed in the general direction they had come from. "Out there."

"You mean to tell me you were riding bare-foot?"

"That's just one of the reasons I can't go traips-ing through the house and up the stairs. I'll leave a trail of mud three feet wide."

"Then come with me."

"I'M MAKING A PUDDLE," Shea said, standing in his kitchen ten minutes later.

"We're making puddles."

"Can I use your sink to wash some of this mud off?"

"I've got a better idea." He grabbed her hand and pulled her down the hall to the bathroom. "Get in the shower."

"What?"

He reached in and turned on the water. "You heard me. Get in the shower."

"Well...thank you for letting me go first—"

"How 'bout together?"

The next thing Shea knew, she was standing un-der the spray of warm water with Reese.

"You're crazy," she squealed.

"Just efficient. Saves time."

"But—"

"Go ahead. Rinse off."

"But—"

He put his hands on either side of her face and tilted her head back. Water sluiced through her hair, carrying away the mud and grime. It felt wonderful and she closed her eyes, giving herself over to the delicious sensation of warmth, water and Reese's touch.

"Hmm. That feels great." When she lifted her head to look at him he was staring at her, hunger burning in his eyes.

"I think…" He took a deep breath. "I think this shower is too small for both of us." He stepped back.

She reached out to him. "But—"

He captured her wrist. "Shea, I want you so much right now I don't think I could be gentle. Do you understand?"

She nodded but didn't fully understand.

"After we're both clean and dry," he said from the other side of the curtain, "we'll pick up where we left off."

She heard the bathroom door click shut a few seconds later. Pick up where they'd left off, he'd said. Meaning before they got the call. Meaning before he had to stop kissing her, touching her breasts.

Shea sighed, the warm water noticeably warmer. Her breasts tingled just thinking about where they'd left off. In fact, her whole body tingled. She began unbuttoning her shirt, knowing she had no dry clothes to wear. Knowing she didn't care.

Reese opened the bathroom door and placed his terry-cloth robe on a nearby hook. Unbuttoning his shirt, he thought back to the moment he had lifted his head and seen her kneeling in the mud beside him. She was crying. It had been raining hard, but he knew she was crying. For him. He had looked into her eyes and seen love. And though no one but his mother had ever really looked at him with love, that's what he'd seen in Shea's eyes. He wasn't sure she realized it or even suspected. He wasn't sure what he was going to do about it. He only knew that the moment he had looked into those killer blue eyes, everything had changed.

The bathroom door creaked open and Shea stepped out. He had been so deep in thought, he hadn't even heard the water cut off.

"Your turn." Her gaze locked with his as she drew the lapels of the robe tighter across her chest. "Thanks for the use of your robe."

"No problem. You want one of my shirts to put on?"

She shook her head, never breaking eye contact. "Hope I didn't use all the hot water."

Reese tried to grin but couldn't quite make it. "I won't be in there long enough to notice." He slipped inside and closed the door.

Shea put her hand over her heart as if that might steady the wild beating.

It didn't.

10

HE CAME OUT of the bathroom ten minutes later wearing a towel wrapped around his lean hips.

Sitting on the sofa, Shea blinked. His hair was still damp from the shower and an occasional drop of water scattered across his broad chest, caught the light as he came toward her. The shoulders she had admired from the first moment she saw him were bare, smooth, tanned and magnificent. *He* was magnificent.

He sat beside her. "Are you cold?"

"What? Oh, uh, just my feet."

He picked up her right foot, propped it on his bare thigh and began rubbing it. "It's a wonder you didn't cut yourself on a rock, running around without shoes in all that mud."

"I guess." The longer he worked, the more her foot seemed to press toward him…toward his… "At the, uh, time, the only thing that seemed important was making sure you didn't drown."

He went to work on her other foot, effectively stretching both of her legs across him. "Thanks, by the way."

"For what?"

"Saving me."

"The horse did all the work."

"Like hell. Where did you learn to do all that, anyway?"

"I've read about similar rescues. And I watched Tyler."

His hands stopped massaging. "You mean tonight? When he pulled me out the first time?"

"Yes."

"You watched him and remembered everything, then did it without missing a beat?"

"What else was I supposed to do? You were in the water and I had to get you out."

Reese looked at her. "I don't know another woman, except possibly Belle, who could have done what you did tonight. You're remarkable."

She ducked her head. "Because I'm smart? That's really nothing special—"

"No." He put a finger under her chin and tilted her head up. "Because you've got guts." His hand touched her cheek. "And heart." Then he smiled. "Did I mention you're also just about the sexiest woman I've ever known?"

"Me? Sexy?" Shea laughed. "You must have gotten some of the muddy water in your head."

"Didn't have any water in my head when we were on the couch a few hours ago. I thought you were sexy then. But…I did have some problems. My mouth was bone-dry. My heart was racing. And my body ached." He moved closer and lowered his head. "For you."

The instant before his lips touched hers, she saw his eyes darken with desire. They were so dark they were almost black. Her lips parted and he kissed her the way he did everything else. With purpose, skill. She half expected the kiss to be hard—instead it was seductively soft, which made it infinitely more powerful. She did the very thing she had said she wouldn't. She melted. If not at his feet, certainly in his arms.

Reese felt her go all warm and soft and deepened the kiss, taking possession of her mouth the way he wanted to take possession of her body. She was so sweet and innocent and hot and hungry, all at the same time. And she was driving him insane with need. He moved, pulling her closer until they were stretched out on the sofa, mouth to mouth. Sex to sex.

"Are we about to pick up where we left off?" she asked breathlessly.

"That's what I had in mind."

She put her hand to the back of his neck. "Good."

"It will be." He was as quick and easy as one of his smiles as he lifted her up and stood with her in his arms. Slowly, he set her feet on the carpet, took her hand and led her to his bedroom.

Shea barely had time to notice the room was done in earth tones with Native American accents before Reese was kissing her again. This time his kiss was urgent, wildly passionate, and it demanded she respond to that passion. She did, gladly. Reaching up, she captured his head between her hands and fit her mouth to his. In doing so, the robe gapped open.

Reese groaned, slipped his hands inside and took full advantage of the opportunity. He had never touched anything so soft in his whole life. She was satin, smooth, warm satin. He ran his hands over her narrow back, down to her hips, then up to her breasts. He filled his hands to over-flowing with her softer-than-soft flesh. Her pale skin, contrasted against his tan fingers, reminded him that she was delicate, to be treasured.

Shea gasped at the contact, then moaned. She actually felt her breasts swell in his hands and be-gin to ache. But it was such a sweet, burning ache. Like before, a cross between pain and pleasure. But now she knew the ultimate cure was his mouth. His hot, demanding mouth. "Touch me...kiss me like before," she begged, letting her arms go back so that the robe slipped off her shoulders and fell to the floor. Eager for the relief only his mouth could bring, she rose up on tiptoes and arched her back. When his lips closed over one of her nipples, they both sighed. But before long Shea's sighs gave way to heavy breathing as he tugged, suckled, licked and even nipped, swirl-ing the pain and pleasure together to the point that she wanted to scream. Mindless with need, she whimpered.

"Did I hurt you?"

"Don't stop," she whispered.

At her words, Reese lost touch with his plan to go easy, to let her set the pace. He lost touch with everything but the need she aroused in him. A need unlike any he'd ever known before. Part physical, part spiritual, it twisted, turned, burned inside him, frightening in its intensity. He tried to slow down, he really did. But holding her was like holding fire in his arms.

"Shea," he said raggedly. "Slow—"

"No." She pressed her hips to him. "I don't

want slow. I've had that all my life. You said I could set the pace, didn't you?"

"Yes."

"Then don't hold back. Make love to me, Reese." She moved her hands to his buttocks and urged him closer. "And don't hold back anything."

He must have gone a little insane after that, because the next thing either of them knew, they were on his bed, naked. He didn't even bother to jerk the covers back.

"Wait," he said, reaching to open a drawer in the bedside table.

Her body was on fire, she couldn't wait. She struggled to sit up, to bring him back to her. "I don't want to— Oh," she said when she saw him tear open the foil-wrapped condom. She hadn't even thought about protection.

Seconds later he was beside her, kissing her, stroking her breasts. She wrapped her arms around his neck, needing him closer. And just when she thought she couldn't stand any more heat, his hand slid between her legs...and turned up the flame.

"Open for me," he urged, his mouth hot on hers.

Restlessly, she shifted her legs and arched her body, granting his request. And was, oh, so sweetly rewarded.

Slowly, delicately, he stroked her tender flesh until she clutched his shoulder. "Reese?"

"Just let it happen, darlin'."

And she did. Twice. Each time her body tensed, the heat building to an unbearable level, and the shuddering release that followed was no release at all because it only stoked the hunger. Finally, his clever fingers drove her up, almost to the peak, but not over. "Please. Oh, Reese, please." She didn't even know what she was begging for, only that he had it, and she wanted it.

He slid his hands beneath her hips to bring her to him, but she met him more than halfway. And as gently as his pounding blood would allow, he slowly, completely filled her. She tensed for half a second, then, with a deep moan, began to move against him, rotating her hips in the ageless dance to a wild rhythm. Harder, faster, until the wildness swept them both up and into a shattering climax. They collapsed in a hot, satisfied heap on the still-made bed.

When his breathing finally slowed, Reese looked down at Shea and smiled. She smiled back.

"You were right," she said, wearing an extremely self-satisfied smile.

"Better than good?"

"Much. Wonderful. Delicious."

"And you moved."

She blushed at the reminder of how quickly she had abandoned herself to passion, but at the same time she was thrilled. "I didn't expect...that is, I never—"

"Well, you have now. And I gotta say, you are one fast learner."

"I've read about techniques."

"You must have a photographic memory."

"Sort of." She glanced away. "As I said, I read a lot, and..." She'd gone this far. It was too late to fumble for words. "Well, is it true that most men want to go to sleep…you know, afterward?"

If it hadn't been for the serious expression on her face, Reese would have laughed. "Are you asking me if I'm sleepy?"

She glanced at the bedside clock. "It is past four in the morning."

"And?"

"Well, I just thought, wondered, actually, if—"

"I wanted to go to sleep."

"Yes."

"No."

She took a deep breath. "Then will you let me know when you feel like…when you're ready to…"

He slid his hand along the outside of one slender leg, then back up the inside until his thumb found her soft folds, still slick with need. "How does now sound?"

THEY SLEPT LATE.

Reese was the first to wake. He stared down at Shea sleeping beside him and was, quite frankly, awed. For a lady with little to no experience, she was the most passionate woman he'd ever known. Last night she had been shy one minute, a seductress the next, a cuddle kitten the next.

And honest through it all.

As a man accustomed to doing the seducing, he'd been a little surprised at first at the way she stated her desire so plainly. He shouldn't have been. Shea was smart enough to know that simply asking was the best way to get what she wanted, and beautiful enough to make it a privilege to give her what she wanted.

Brains, beauty and passion. Shea Alexander could keep a man busy for a lifetime.

A lifetime?

When had he started thinking in those terms?

And others, like…forever….happily ever after. The kind of words he had avoided most of his life, particularly where women were concerned. Just like he had avoided…

He glanced at Shea again. Her lips were slightly parted as she slept, her hand rested on his shoulder. Was what he felt love? This longing to be near her, to touch her. Was that love? In the past, he would have labeled it lust, but after last night… What they'd shared had gone way beyond lust. He had never felt about anyone the way he felt about Shea. He wanted to protect her. Pamper her, fight with her, make love, make babies, love her until…

He loved her.

The admission shocked him momentarily, then he remembered something Cade had told him. *I'd never been in love before, so I wasn't sure how I was supposed to feel…. It had been Belle all along. I was just too stubborn to admit it.*

Reese ran a hand over a darkly stubbled chin. When the hell had all this happened? he wondered. As soon as the question formed in his mind, the answer was there, clear and undeniable. It must have been happening since the first time he saw her, but the defining moment had been last night. In the mud. Shea on her knees beside him.

Thanking God that he was all right.

He had looked into her eyes and known she belonged to him, and he to her. In that instant, he knew he wasn't alone anymore. The emptiness left behind when his mother had abandoned him was filled up. He trusted her with his love, his heart, his soul.

It *had* been Shea all along. And he *had* been too stubborn to admit what was happening to him. They had started out fighting like—what had Cade said, two cats in the same bag—and ended up in the same bed. And always she met him on equal terms. Making love or making wine. This kind of woman—this chance for happiness—came along once in a lifetime, and he'd be damned if he would let his pride blow it for him.

The sixty-four-thousand-dollar question was how she felt about him. Yes, they had gone way beyond mere lovemaking last night, but not once did she say anything about love. Only need.

Not that he could blame her—he hadn't said anything either. He had promised himself he would give her soft words and romance, but then she was all heat and heaven in his arms, and the promise incinerated in the middle of their passion. But she had never given him even the slightest indication that she wanted anything more than sex. What if that was all she wanted?

Reese shivered, suddenly chilled through. Now that he knew he loved Shea, that he wanted to spend the rest of his life with her, the thought that she might not return that love was more painful than he could have imagined.

He had to know how she felt.

Careful not to wake her, he eased himself out of

bed. She sighed, snuggling down under the covers, and he had to stifle the urge to kiss her awake and proclaim his love. He felt happy, excited and anxious all at the same time. He wanted to share all of it—and keep it to himself like a sweet secret. This love business was confusing, to say the least. Maybe his thinking would be clearer after a cup of coffee. He grabbed a pair of jeans on the way out the door.

Coffee was definitely the first order of the day, he thought, stepping into his pants. Nope, make that second. The first was to find out how young Chance and his parents were doing. Unfortunately, he wasn't able to speak with Cade or Belle when he called, but a helpful nurse informed him that the baby was still breathing on his own and doing very well.

"Good morning."

He turned to find Shea wearing his robe and standing several feet away. "Morning, Bright Eyes. I've got some good news for you," he said, coming toward her.

"Chance?"

"Yep. He's doin' great."

"Oh, Reese." She threw her arms around him. "That's wonderful. I'm so relieved."

"I knew you would be. And speaking of wonderful..." His lips brushed hers in a feather-soft kiss. "You are."

"You're pretty terrific yourself."

"What happened to wonderful?"

"Okay, wonderful, sexy, handsome—"

"Aw, go on. No, I mean it. Don't stop. Go on."

Shea put her forehead to his chest and laughed. "Incorrigible, vain—"

"Whoa. Back up."

"To wonderful?"

"To this." He lowered his mouth to hers, only this time the kiss wasn't soft. It was hot, hard and deep. Exactly the way he wanted to be inside her. Exactly the way he was, not three minutes later.

They missed coffee, breakfast *and* lunch.

By early afternoon, when Reese walked her to the main house and left her with a bone-melting kiss to remember him by, Shea was weak from love in more ways than one. Her body would rebound with rest. She wasn't so sure about her heart.

She sighed, sliding farther into the tub of deliciously warm water she'd been soaking in for the last twenty minutes. She picked up a bath sponge and squeezed floral-scented water over her shoulders. "You wanted experience. Well, you got it. Now what are you going to do?"

Love Reese, she thought. And keep on loving him. As if she had a choice. She'd given him her heart as well as her body and couldn't reclaim either. Nor did she want to. What she wanted was for him to love her back. In all her life she had never known such closeness with anyone, not even her parents. And she was almost positive he felt it, too. But "almost" wasn't good enough.

She knew Reese had been a loner most of his life. They had that much in common. If he was anything like her, being alone had made dealing with feelings that much harder, much less expressing them. Maybe he needed time to get used to the idea of being with her, making love, loving. Maybe they had to put the cart before the horse, so to speak, but who was to say they couldn't arrive at the desired destination all the same? They had time. She had time to let him know how much she loved him. Time to let him love her.

As plans went, it wasn't monumental, but it was simple and from her heart.

THEY DROVE into Sweetwater Springs that afternoon to get a gift for the baby and pick up some flowers for Belle.

"How 'bout I buy you the best steak you've ever eaten after we leave the hospital?" Reese offered, guiding his truck into a parking space on the north side of the courthouse.

"Sounds heavenly. I can't wait."

"Then we'll take in a movie." *No*, he reminded himself. *Don't tell her. Let her choose.* "Or we can do whatever you want to do."

"Does that fireplace in your cabin work?" she asked. The thought of making love in firelight was so romantic.

"Yeah." Images of the two of them naked in front of the fireplace streaked across his mind, leaving a trail of smoke.

"Then could we maybe…just go back to your place and have a fire?"

"A fire is fine. Yeah. We can do that." He got out, walked around the truck and helped her out, hoping she didn't notice his hand trembling slightly.

"So, are you coming with me to pick out a gift for little Chance, or shall we split up?"

"Let's split up. You do your shopping, I'll get the flowers, and we'll meet back at the truck."

"All right. But our timing may not click. I, uh, need to go to the post office and buy some stamps."

"No problem. I'll wait for you. I need to mail a letter anyway."

"Oh, well..." Shea hedged. "You know how women are when they start drooling over baby clothes. Don't wait on me."

"Okay. See ya in a while."

Shea started off for the only department store in town, then glanced over her shoulder. Thank goodness, she thought. It looked as if Reese were headed for the post office. At least she could stop worrying about running into him. Tomorrow, or the next day, she would have to write to *Texas Men* magazine and ask them not to forward any more letters to her. Then she would write to all of her subjects and tell them...what?

The truth. That she had found the man of her dreams.

On the other side of the square, Reese decided to stop at the florist shop before going to the post office. The lady behind the counter was thrilled to hear the good news about the McBride baby and helped him select a floral arrangement that would barely fit on the seat between him and Shea. That was all right. Nothing but the biggest and the best for Mama, Papa and baby. But the arrangement was so large that he had to put it in the truck, then go to the post office.

He had just unloaded the flowers and locked

the door to his truck when Smitty Lewis hailed him.

"Hey, there, Reese. How ya doin'?"

"Can't complain. How you boys doin'?" He nodded to Alvin Delworthy and Old Walt.

"Say, heard the news," Alvin said. "Bet Cade is so proud he's near to bustin' his britches."

"Yeah. He and Belle are sure happy."

Old Walt set his whittling aside. "Young'uns are a blessin', and that's a fact."

"Like you ever married and had kids," Alvin accused.

"I got eyes, ain't I? I can sure as hell see how folks love their kids, can't I?"

Grinning, Smitty hitched up his baggy jeans. "Say, that there new lady of yours is shore a looker."

Reese couldn't help but smile. "Shea's a beautiful woman, all right. And smart."

"Yeah, we seen her when she come into town a few days back."

"Blowin' hard that day," Alvin said.

"That's a fact."

Smitty pushed his hat far enough back to scratch his head. "Beats me, though, why a purdy woman like that would write to one of them, you know, racy magazines."

"Racy?" Reese asked.

"Sure 'nough." Smitty turned to Alvin. "You 'member that big ol' envelope that blowed clean across the courthouse lawn."

"Ought to," Alvin replied. "I caught it and give it back to her. It was from one of them magazines with the personals ads. What did I tell you that label said?" He looked at the others.

"*Texas Men*," Old Walt answered. "Shameless, if you ask me. Woman like that writing to strange men."

Reese shook his head. "You must be mistaken."

"Nope. Seen it myself. Label stuck up on the corner, big as life."

"Wait a minute. Are you telling me that Shea Alexander got an envelope from *Texas Men* magazine?"

"You deaf, boy? Ain't that what Alvin just told you?"

Confused, Reese couldn't think of any reason for Shea to receive mail from the magazine unless...

Unless she had answered an ad.

But that didn't make any sense. Why would an intelligent, attractive woman like Shea want to write to a total stranger? Maybe for the same reason he did?

"Well now, why don't you just go ask her yourself." Smitty pointed across the street. "She's walkin' in the post office right now."

Reese glanced up to see Shea disappear into the building. He didn't know what the hell was going on, but he intended to find out. "Thanks," he told the three. "I believe I'll do just that."

Across the street at the post office, Shea unlocked her mailbox, pulled out the large envelope and ripped it open. Inside were at least a dozen letters, including one from Mr. Serious. Now what? she wondered. She couldn't very well waltz up to Reese with this envelope tucked under her arm. What if he saw the return address? He might not ask about it, but he would certainly wonder. What kind of explanation could she give for receiving mail from *Texas Men* magazine other than the obvious?

Making a quick decision, she wadded up the envelope and threw it in a nearby trash bin. Stuffing the letters into the side pocket of her purse, she turned to leave and ran into Reese. Literally. The jarring collision caused her to drop her purse.

"Whoa." He put out a hand to steady her.

But it was too late. When her purse landed, the letters slid out, scattering across the floor.

Naturally, being a gentleman, Reese knelt down and began scooping them up. "Looks like you've got a lot of pen pals." He handed her a stack, then squatted to pick up the rest.

"No, not really."

He reached out, collecting the last two letters as he stood up. "Here you go." She grasped one envelope but he held the other back—the one from Mr. Serious. "Where did you get this letter?"

"It's from a friend of mine in Austin. Just a girl I work with." She reached for it, but he moved it away. And he was staring at her with such an odd expression on his face. She held out her hand for her mail. He just kept staring. "Reese?"

"Where did you get this letter?"

"I just told you—"

"You're lying."

Shea blinked. His voice was so cold. "I—I beg your—"

"This isn't from a girl you work with. It's a response to a personals ad in a magazine."

"Why would you think such a thing?"

"Because I wrote it."

"What?"

"You heard me. *I* wrote this letter."

11

"THAT'S..." Shea shook her head. "That's not possible."

"The hell it's not. Don't you think I recognize my own handwriting?"

"But that would mean you're Mr. Serious. It's not possible. I mean, that would just be too..."

"Weird."

"Yes."

"I think we passed weird a couple of minutes ago, so I'd really appreciate an explanation of how you got this letter."

"I—I..." The truth was going to sound ludicrous, but no more so than Reese saying he was Mr. Serious. Now, *that* was ludicrous. "I, uh... well, I happened across this magazine. Quite by accident, really. I mean, it's not the kind of thing I normally... Oh, this is going to sound so ridiculous you'll probably think I've lost my mind or— wait a minute. You couldn't be Mr. Serious unless..." Her mouth fell open as she looked at the letter in his hand, then at him, a light finally dawning. "*You* put an ad in *Texas Men* magazine?"

Reese glanced around. "Keep it down, will you?" He grabbed her hand and practically dragged her out of the post office. "You don't have to announce it to the whole world," he told her when they were outside and out of earshot of anyone else entering the building.

"Ohmygod, you did! I can't believe it. Why? You're smart, handsome and incredibly sexy. You must have women standing in line just dying to go out with you. Why would you, of all people, take out a personals ad?"

He shrugged. "Even us smart, handsome, incredibly sexy men get lonely. Aren't we entitled to happiness?"

"Of course, I just meant that you don't look like you need help finding a woman."

"I thought I did. Watching Cade and Belle every day, seeing what they had together...the love and the trust. I wanted that. And believe it or not, there are still a lot of women who might think it's exciting to take a half-breed to bed, but not to wed. And there are a lot of dishonest ones. I wanted more than a one-night stand, so...I enlisted a little help. And for a little while I wrote to a woman I thought was special." He ran a hand up and down her arm. "But then you came along, and like it or not, I was done for. I know this isn't the time or place, but..." He took a deep breath. "I love you, Shea."

Stunned, her heart nearly bursting with love for him, she simply stared.

"Look, I know you're used to men in thousand-dollar suits, not cowboys in faded jeans. And we come from different backgrounds, but I do love you. I want you to marry me."

Right there, in front of the post office, in front of anyone who happened to be in downtown Sweetwater Springs, he kissed her, long and thoroughly. When he ended the kiss, he waited for her answer.

Shea looked into Reese's dark eyes, filled with love and trust.

Trust.

Would he trust her after he found out she was Natalie? Maybe she could pretend... No. She couldn't lie to him. She'd done enough of that. Ironic, she thought. She had been lying to the man she loved without knowing it.

Reese glanced around and noticed several people had stopped to take in the scene. "C'mon," he said, taking her arm. "We could stand a little more privacy."

They went back to his truck. Inside, Reese set the bouquet of flowers on the floor and turned to her. "Sorry. I hadn't intended for everything to be so public. This is the first time I've ever asked a woman to marry me, so I'm not real sure about the rules. Aren't you supposed to say something? Like yes?" When he saw tears fill her eyes, a cold dread clutched at his heart. "Shea? What is it? Is something wrong?"

"Oh, Reese," she whispered. "I love you so much. I never thought...never dreamed..."

Relieved, he felt a smile wreathe his face. Still holding the letter in one hand, he hauled her into his arms. "Hey, that's nothing to cry about. For a second there, you scared me. I thought you might say no."

She hugged him tight. Hugged him as if it might be her last time to touch him, hold him. "Reese..."

"What is it, Bright Eyes?" He wiped away a tear.

"About the letter…"

"Oh, that's right." He drew back and looked into her eyes. "You didn't tell me why you answered my ad. By the way, that magazine is slow as Christmas sending your mail. This—" he held up the letter "—must be at least a month old. I only wrote to one woman after the first batch of responses."

Shea felt as if she were standing on the edge of a cliff, about to plunge to her doom. Not a bad analogy, she thought. She would be doomed without Reese, and she very much feared that might happen.

"So how did—" Reese glanced at the postmark. "This was postmarked last week." For the first time he gave his full attention to the "number" address the magazine assigned to all correspondents. "But this is—"

"Addressed to number 8059. I'm Natalie."

"I don't understand."

But he was beginning to. She could see it in his eyes.

"I…I picked five men out of the magazine to correspond—"

"Five?"

"Yes. I thought that would be a good number for the purpose of my experiment. You see, I…I've never dated much. I don't know how to flirt or make casual conversation with men. Then I found the magazine and came up with this idea for a kind of…" She hesitated. How could an idea that had sounded so brilliant in the beginning now sound so incredibly stupid? "Correspondence school. I planned to write to the men and learn how to deal with them on paper before I tried it for real."

"And Natalie?"

She swallowed hard, knowing how cold all of this might sound, praying for his understanding. "I made her up. A fantasy I've had ever since I was in junior high school."

"You lied."

"Yes," she whispered, and waited. She heard the pain, felt the heat of his anger. She should have known his pride had to be defended. She only hoped that they could get past it.

His hand dropped from her shoulder. "So, I was just part of your experiment."

"I didn't know it was you. How could I? You know the magazine doesn't give out real names and addresses. I only knew you as Mr. Serious."

"And you never intended anything to come of your letters. You weren't interested in a relationship, just information."

"No!" She almost reached for him but stopped herself. Begging would only make matters worse. "I wanted a relationship. That's why I answered the ad in the first place. And just like you, I wanted what Belle and Cade had. I wanted to find a man and fall in love. I just didn't know how to—"

"Do it honestly." The coldness in his voice was like a slap in the face.

"Reese, please. Try to understand."

"I understand you thought you were so smart you could manipulate people and it didn't matter. What about the sex, Shea? Was that just part of your education?"

"No. I made love to you because I wanted to. Because I love you."

"What I don't understand is how I could have been so gullible. Lord knows I've met enough users in my life. Can't believe I didn't see through you."

"I didn't—"

"Save it."

"Reese—"

He held up his hand to silence her. "We can't go see Belle now. She'll know there's something wrong the minute we walk in the door."

"I know."

He headed back to the ranch. Not one word was exchanged between them until he pulled up in front of the house, got out and opened her door.

"What about the flowers?"

"Leave 'em. I'll take them to Belle later. If one of us doesn't show up, she'll get worried."

Obviously, he didn't intend for it to be her. "What excuse will you give her about me?"

He glanced away. "I don't know. Can't think right now."

Her heart was already shattered. "Reese, I know I've hurt you, but can't you accept that it was unintentional? I answered that ad for the same reason you wrote it. I was lonely. I needed someone."

"You knew you had lied and you let me go on making a fool out of myself right there in front of the whole town."

"Is that what this is all about. Your pride?"

"It's about the fact that you lied to me. That I thought you were one kind of person and you turned out to be another."

Maybe her pride kicked in at that moment, but she realized he didn't want to understand. "No, Reese. I'm the same person. The person that loves you. I haven't used you, I've loved you. And I want to go on loving you."

"Don't."

"You don't have any say in the matter. Fool that I am, I'll probably go on loving you for the rest of my life. And you know something? It hurts. It'll go on hurting for a long time, but you are the one I feel sorry for, not me. Because now that I know what it's like to love, I'm not going to spend the rest of my life without it."

"You're not the person I thought you were."

"Then I guess you should consider yourself lucky you found out in time to avoid making a terrible mistake. You were right from the beginning. I'm not your type, remember?"

"Wish to hell I had remembered."

It was the final, painful blow. With the few tatters of dignity she still had, Shea walked into the house and closed the door. Rationally, she knew her feet were on solid ground. Emotionally, she had tumbled off that cliff into darkness.

WEARING HIS BEST SMILE, Reese sailed into Belle's hospital room carrying the flowers. "Here you go. How's that for a big bunch of flowers?"

"Impressive." Belle glanced behind him. "Where's Shea?"

"She, uh, wasn't feeling too well."

Belle automatically reached for the phone. "No, don't call her," Reese insisted. "She had a whopper of a headache and said she was going to take something and lie down for a while. She'll call you when she wakes up."

"Oh…okay." She smiled. "Did you go by the nursery?"

"Of course."

"Isn't Chance the best-looking baby in there?"

"Unquestionably. Say, where's that worthless husband of yours?"

"He's gone undercover."

"What?"

"He's going to try and smuggle an order of french fries in to me. I haven't had junk food since my doctor cut me off almost four months ago. And I'm really craving french fries."

"What if he's caught?"

"I've got bail money."

"I promise not to squeal on you."

Despite the banter, Belle had been watching him closely ever since he arrived. Reese didn't think he could fool her for long.

"So, you want to tell me what's wrong?"

"What makes you think anything is wrong? The winery is running smooth as silk. No problems at the ranch—"

"Tyler called."

"Oh, well. Dolly took her usual wild ride and I had to go drag her home."

"Tyler said Shea pulled you out of a bad situation."

"Tyler talks too much."

"I also heard from Posey that Shea didn't sleep in the main house last night."

"What have you got going? A network of spies?"

"No. Just concerned friends. Reese?"

"What?"

"You know I couldn't care more about you if you were my brother, but Shea's fragile in a way. If you've hurt her—"

"Fragile? Oh, yeah. Shea Alexander is about as fragile as a pit bull."

"What's going on?"

"Not one damned thing. Not anymore."

"But there was."

All his resentment boiled to the surface, blowing like Old Faithful. "Do you know what she did? She conducted an experiment with men! Five of them. She got names out of a magazine and started writing to them so she could educate herself on how to handle a man. How's that for fragile?"

"Uh—"

"And get this. She lied to every one of those men. Told them she was a sweet little kindergarten teacher just looking for romance."

"Well…"

"Well, what?"

"Well, what I don't understand is why you're so outraged. She didn't lie to you," Belle said.

"The hell she didn't." The minute he said the words, he wished he hadn't.

"I think I'm beginning to understand."

"Understand what?" Cade asked, coming through the door.

Belle's eyes lit up. "Did you get them?"

"Would I let you down, darlin'?" He pulled a paper bag from beneath his shirt. "What are we understanding?"

Belle practically dived into the french fries. "That Reese put an ad in that magazine you told me about, and guess who answered it?"

"Who?"

"Shea."

Cade turned to his friend. "You're kiddin' me."

"Wish to hell I was," Reese mumbled.

"You really sent in an ad?"

"Look," Reese told them. "It doesn't make any difference. The damage is done. I thought Shea was one kind of person and she turned out to be another. So we had a fling. That's all it was. Maybe I thought it could be more, but she ruined it. And she can just swing her little butt back to Austin for all I care. As a matter of fact, that would suit me just fine considering the fool I made out of myself."

Cade looked at his wife and raised an eyebrow.

"But I know you need her to stay and help. Well, I can handle that. I don't have to work side by side with the woman. We'll work it out somehow just so long as I don't have to deal with her lies—"

"Uh, Reese?"

He glanced at Cade, who jerked his head toward Belle. A very angry-looking Belle.

"Now, darlin', you're not supposed to get upset. Think about Chance comin' in here to nurse in a little while—"

"You're a coward, Reese Barrett."

"Belle—"

"You heard me. As long as I've known you, you've come up with an excuse to dump every woman you've dated. They're either too pushy or too weak, too loose with their morals or not loose enough, too tight with money or too free. They're always too something."

"What did I tell ya?" Cade added. "Too picky."

"And too scared to face the truth."

"Which is, according to you?" Reese demanded.

"That you'd rather stay lonely than risk getting hurt. Risk trusting someone to love you the way you want to be loved. It's hard for you to trust, Reese. I can say that because I was the same way. And I almost lost Cade because of my pride." She shoved the half-eaten french fries away. "The irony of the situation is that, in her own way, Shea is just like you. She's spent her whole life lonely, thinking no man would want her, as is. So she tried to change that, using the only tool she thought she had—her brains. At least she had the guts to try."

"She's right, partner."

Reese looked into the faces of his friends and didn't know how to respond. He'd come in here thinking his anger was justified, and somehow they had turned it around. He probably trusted these two people more than anyone else in the world. They cared enough to tell him the truth even when he didn't like it. Were they right? Had he let his pride take over, when deep in his heart he knew Shea hadn't set out to hurt him?

"Maybe," was all he said. Then he walked out, feeling Belle's eyes on him as he left.

He was still rolling everything around in his head when he climbed into his truck and saw the letter stuck in the seat. He picked it up, started to toss it into the trash bin mounted underneath the dashboard, then changed his mind. Instead, he opened the letter and read it.

SHEA PARKED the shiny red Suburban in front of the motel room and took out her overnight bag. She couldn't stay at the ranch, but she hadn't gone far. Just to the edge of Lubbock and the first decent-looking motel. Later she would telephone the hospital and talk to Belle. She would explain that Reese had been part of the ranch long before she came. He belonged there and she was the outsider.

Besides nursing her broken heart, she now had to deal with disappointing her best friend. She had promised Belle she'd help with the business, and she would find a way to keep that promise. But it would have to be long-distance, because she couldn't bear the thought of seeing Reese day in and day out. It was one thing to have her heart broken. Seeing him and never being able to touch him or kiss him would kill what was left of her spirit. For a woman with such a high IQ, she had certainly managed to do some dumb things.

Like fall in love with Reese?

No, that wasn't dumb. Right now it was agony, but never dumb.

Tired, emotionally wrung out, she locked the motel room door behind her, fell onto the bed and let the tears fall.

She cried herself to sleep, dreaming of Reese. Dreaming of the two of them riding off together on magnificent horses. Riding, riding, the horse's hooves pounding across the range, pounding...pounding...

Shea woke up to a pounding on her door.

Sleepy, she staggered to the door and opened it. "Reese?"

"Can I come in?"

"I don't think so. Natalie's not here."

"I don't want Natalie." She started to close the door, but he stopped her. "She's not my type."

"What?"

He pushed his way in. "I said she's not my type. Not anymore."

"But I thought—"

"You probably thought I was a real son of a bitch, but we'll discuss that later. Right now, I want you to read this letter." He handed her the envelope addressed to number 8059.

She shook her head.

"Then I'll read it to you.

"'Dear Natalie,

This will be my last letter. I've enjoyed writing to you, but I think it's only fair to tell you that I've met someone special.

I wanted you to know because I don't think it would have happened if you hadn't answered my ad. You see, I have trouble trusting new people. I know it comes from struggling with my Cherokee heritage, but knowing that hasn't made it any easier. The truth is, I haven't trusted a woman since my mother left us—her Cherokee husband and her ten-year-old half-breed son. But your letters have helped me. Maybe it was because I felt such a strong connection to you from the first, or maybe it was the fact that sharing my feelings on paper was less of a risk. Whatever the reason, you were kind and understanding, and I will always think of you as a friend.

The lady I've found is like you in some ways. She's caring and honest. She's also got a stubborn streak that I've come to respect. I guess what I'm trying to say is that she might not be what I expected, but she's everything I want. And there's someone just as special out there for you. When you find him, please tell him for me that he's a very lucky man.'"

Reese folded the letter and stuck it in his pocket. "I wrote this, but I had forgotten the contents until today. I was a lucky man. Now I only want to know one thing."

When Shea lifted her head, tears were streaming down her face. "What's that?" she whispered.

"Can you forgive me? If you can't, I'll accept that for now, but don't expect me to give up."

"Give up?"

"C'mon, Bright Eyes. You know I can match you beat for beat when it comes to stubborn. If I'm determined to have you forgive me, I'll hound you until you do."

"But I…"

"Please, Shea." He reached out and touched her cheek. "Just let me love you."

"Oh, Reese," she whispered, throwing her arms around his neck. "There's nothing to forgive. I just want to love you and have you love me right back."

Reese pulled back and tucked a strand of hair

behind her ear. "I can't believe it. After all this time, we've finally agreed on something."

Shea grinned. "I wouldn't get used to it, cowboy."

_____Epilogue_____

Six months later

SHEA AND BELLE, holding a wiggly Chance, stood in the shade of a huge live oak tree at the corner of the McBride patio as guests at the baby's christening enjoyed wine and a catered buffet. Everyone for miles around had been invited, and judging from the smiling faces, the party was definitely a success. As Shea glanced around she realized many of the people she had considered Reese's, Belle's and Cade's friends were now her friends, as well. For the first time in her life she felt totally accepted. Her life in Austin now seemed light-years away from her place in this close-knit, caring community that felt like family. And all of it was courtesy of her love for Reese.

Shea Alexander Barrett sighed, realizing that for all her intelligence, she had never known the true meaning of contentment until now. She was loved, happy and contented.

At that moment Alvin, Smitty and Old Walt strolled by, their plates loaded. They all tipped their hats. "Mighty nice spread," Alvin commented.

"Woulda made your granddaddy proud, and that's a fact," Old Walt stated to Belle.

Belle waved. "Thanks. Enjoy yourselves."

"Can I hold Chance?" Shea asked.

"You don't even have to ask. After all, you're his godmother."

Shea picked up the baby and held him close. "He's grown so much."

"I know." Belle touched her son's hair. "Sometimes when I look at him and see how robust he is, I have trouble remembering that he was so tiny and frail at birth."

"But he's healthy now." Shea tickled Chance's tummy. "Aren't you, sweetie. And such a good baby."

"That's quite a picture."

The women looked up to find their husbands coming toward them, accompanied by Devlin O'Brian. "Yes, sir," Devlin went on. "The two most beautiful women in the county and the best-looking kid. I'd say you boys did all right."

"All right?" Cade looked at Reese. "Sounds like the understatement of the year."

"Try the decade." Reese put his arm around Shea's waist. She smiled up at him and his heart raced from a jolt of pure joy. Her beauty was a given as far as he was concerned, not just because she had a lovely face and form, but because she had a lovely and loving spirit, as well. Now, gazing up at him with a baby in her arms, she had never seemed more beautiful. The only thing that would make the picture more perfect would be if she was holding their child.

"You look real natural holding a baby," Dev said as Cade took Chance from her.

Shea pulled her gaze from Reese. "Thanks."

"Glad you could make the christening, Dev," Belle said.

"Wouldn't have missed it. Too bad the rest of the old gang didn't show."

"We haven't even heard from Logan Walker," Belle commented. "Cade said he's probably up to his eyebrows in some case and hasn't opened his mail, much less checked his answering machine."

"Sounds like Logan." Dev smiled at Chance and the baby seemed fascinated by the stranger.

"Doesn't it?" Cade said. "Sloane called. He's flying home from South America in a few months for good, so he couldn't get time off."

"They'll show up when you least expect them." Dev extended a finger to Chance, who immediately grabbed it and tried to bring it to his mouth. "That's it, kid. Go for what you want."

"Don't encourage him. He's too much like Cade already."

"Doesn't look like it did Cade any harm. He wound up with you, didn't he?"

Belle actually blushed. "You are shameless, Devlin O'Brian."

"So they tell me. You know," he said to his friends, "you two ornery cowboys are downright lucky. But I've gotta tell you, all these weddings and this christening are making me nervous."

Cade laughed. "Too close for comfort, huh?"

"Yeah. Think I'll find me some adventure before another one of Belle's good-looking friends comes along."

"Be careful," Belle warned. "You may run so fast you'll get caught."

"I'm always careful." With a wink he sauntered

off in the direction of a tall blonde with incredibly long legs.

Reese and Cade exchanged looks over their wives' heads. Looks that said more clearly than words that they didn't envy their friend's single existence one bit.

Chance began to fret and rub his eyes. "Naptime for you, young man," his mother announced.

Cade kissed his son's cheek. "See you later, buddy," he said as mother and child headed for the house. He turned to Reese and Shea. "Guess we should mingle, huh?"

"If you don't mind, Cade," Shea said, "I think I'll beg off."

Instantly concerned, Reese looked into his wife's face. "You okay?"

"Of course. I'm just really tired."

"Well, I guess so," Cade said. "You worked on this shindig every bit as hard as Belle. Both of you, get outta here."

They said their goodbyes and walked toward their cabin.

"You could do with a nap," Reese said. "I wasn't going to mention it, but you do look a little pale lately. You and Belle went all out for this party."

"Oh, planning the party was fun. Actually, I have a confession to make."

"Uh-oh. Married only five months and already making confessions. Some rake's stolen your heart. What's his name? I'll challenge him to a duel."

"Chance McBride, but that's not my confession. I just said I was tired so we could be alone."

He dipped his head to kiss her. "You read my mind."

"Hmm." She sighed, giving herself over to the thrill of kissing him, knowing he would still have this effect on her fifty years from now. "Let's drive up to the house," she said. Fifteen minutes later, Reese braked his truck at the construction site of their new home.

They had spent the last three months revising floor plans until they were satisfied their home would be perfect. Reese was functioning as general contractor, Shea as the financial manager. They had walked the property Cade and Belle had sold them almost every day for a month after their quiet wedding, dreaming of the kind of house they wanted to build. Now the dream was becoming a reality.

As soon as they stopped, Shea took some fabric swatches out of a bag and spread them on the hood of the truck, then stepped back so Reese could see.

"So, what do you think?"

Reese stepped up behind her, slipped his arms around her waist and pulled her against him. "I think you're the prettiest, smartest woman I know."

"And I'm flattered, but—"

He nibbled her ear. "Did I forget to add sexy? And good enough to eat?"

"That's not…oh, ah…what I'm talking about."

"Talking isn't what I had in mind."

Shea sighed. "Oh, well…" He had almost completely unbuttoned her blouse before she remembered her mission. "Oh no, you don't." She turned in his arms, put her hands on his shoulders and moved him away. "A few more of your kisses and I'll forget my name, much less what I wanted to tell you."

He grinned. "C'mere, Nameless."

"Now, Reese." She took a step back. "This is important."

"Nothing is more important than kissing you."

He reached for her and she took another step back. "Not until you give me your opinion."

"Thought I just did. Beautiful, brainy and mouthwatering. Now, stand still."

"Not me." She pointed to the fabric swatches. "Those."

"What the hell are they?"

"I'm trying to select a color scheme for our bedroom and I want your opinion."

Reese eyed the fabric and shook his head. "The crew I hired only started framing our house two days ago. I think we've got a little time to decide."

"Wrong, cowboy. It takes weeks, even months, to order fabric, have window treatments and bed coverings made."

"You decide."

"Uh-uh. We're doing this together, remember? Besides, I honestly want your—" Being hauled into his arms cut her off.

"Bright Eyes, I don't care what our bedroom looks like as long as there's a big bed and we're in it." He went back to nuzzling her neck.

"What about the rest of the house?"

"Same thing. A bed in every room."

"Even the nursery?"

Reese drew back and looked into her eyes. "Did you say nursery?"

"We've talked about having children."

"Yeah." He lifted a wayward strand of hair from her cheek. "And we said maybe in a year."

"You still feel that way?"

"Would you be upset if I changed my mind?"

Shea held her breath and a tiny knot of anxiety twisted inside her. "What…what do you mean?"

"When I saw you holding Chance today, I wanted you to be holding our child. I really want that, Shea." He closed his eyes. "So much my heart aches. Would you be upset if we had children sooner than we planned?" When he opened his eyes, she was crying.

For a split second Shea saw his childhood fear in his eyes and put a finger to his lips before he could speak. There was nothing she could do to remove the pain his own mother had inflicted by abandoning him, but she could love away his fear. "How soon?"

He smiled now. "We could start today. Build a family as we build our home."

Shea raised herself up on tiptoe and looped her arms around his neck. "You're too late… Daddy."

He blinked. "Daddy? You mean…are you…are we?"

"We most certainly are."

"When?"

"In about eight months."

Reese clasped her to him, then swung her up and around in a circle. A deliriously happy circle. He was totally in love, his heart and soul captured by this petite, bright-eyed woman who had first turned his life upside down, then right side up. More right than it had ever been. And now a child to share made that life complete. He had been alone for so long, a lone wolf resigned to a solitary existence. Now the lone wolf had found his mate.

Catch more great

 HARLEQUIN™ Movies

featured on the movie channel tmc

Premiering July 11th
Another Woman
Starring Justine Bateman and
Peter Outerbridge
Based on the novel by Margot Dalton

Don't miss next month's movie!
Premiering August 8th
The Waiting Game
Based on the novel by *New York Times*
bestselling author Jayne Ann Krentz

If you are not currently a subscriber to
The Movie Channel, simply call your
local cable or satellite provider for more
details. Call today, and don't miss out
on the romance!

the movie channel tmc   HARLEQUIN®

100% pure movies.
100% pure fun.

Makes any time special ™

Harlequin, Joey Device, Makes any time special and Superromance are trademarks of
Harlequin Enterprises Limited. The Movie Channel is a service mark of Showtime Networks, Inc.,
a Viacom Company.

An Alliance Television Production

PHMBPA798

Take 2 bestselling love stories FREE

Plus get a FREE surprise gift!

Special Limited-Time Offer

Mail to Harlequin Reader Service®

3010 Walden Avenue
P.O. Box 1867
Buffalo, N.Y. 14240-1867

YES! Please send me 2 free Harlequin Temptation® novels and my free surprise gift. Then send me 4 brand-new novels every month, which I will receive before they appear in bookstores. Bill me at the low price of $3.12 each plus 25¢ delivery and applicable sales tax, if any.* That's the complete price, and a saving of over 10% off the cover prices—quite a bargain! I understand that accepting the books and gift places me under no obligation ever to buy any books. I can always return a shipment and cancel at any time. Even if I never buy another book from Harlequin, the 2 free books and the surprise gift are mine to keep forever.

142 HEN CH7G

Name	(PLEASE PRINT)	
Address		Apt. No.
City	State	Zip

This offer is limited to one order per household and not valid to present Harlequin Temptation® subscribers. *Terms and prices are subject to change without notice. Sales tax applicable in N.Y.

UTEMP-98

©1990 Harlequin Enterprises Limited

DEBBIE MACOMBER

invites you to the

HEART OF TEXAS

Join Debbie Macomber as she brings you the lives
and loves of the folks in the ranching community
of Promise, Texas.

If you loved Midnight Sons—don't miss
Heart of Texas! A brand-new six-book series
from Debbie Macomber.

Available in February 1998
at your favorite retail store.

Heart of Texas by Debbie Macomber

Lonesome Cowboy	February '98
Texas Two-Step	March '98
Caroline's Child	April '98
Dr. Texas	May '98
Nell's Cowboy	June '98
Lone Star Baby	July '98

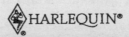

HARLEQUIN®

MEN at WORK

All work and no play?
Not these men!

July 1998

MACKENZIE'S LADY by Dallas Schulze

Undercover agent Mackenzie Donahue's
lazy smile and deep blue eyes were his best
weapons. But after rescuing—and kissing!—
damsel in distress Holly Reynolds, how could
he betray her by spying on her brother?

August 1998

MISS LIZ'S PASSION by Sherryl Woods

Todd Lewis could put up a building with ease,
but quailed at the sight of a classroom! Still,
Liz Gentry, his son's teacher, was no battle-ax,
and soon Todd started planning some
extracurricular activities of his own....

September 1998

A CLASSIC ENCOUNTER
by Emilie Richards

Doctor Chris Matthews was intelligent, sexy
and *very* good with his hands—which made
him all the more dangerous to single mom
Lizette St. Hilaire. So how long could she
resist Chris's special brand of TLC?

Available at your favorite retail outlet!

MEN AT WORK™

Look us up on-line at: http://www.romance.net

PMAW2

Not The Same Old Story!

 Exciting, glamorous romance stories that take readers around the world.

 Sparkling, fresh and tender love stories that bring you pure romance.

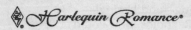 Bold and adventurous— Temptation is strong women, bad boys, great sex!

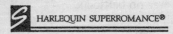 Provocative and realistic stories that celebrate life and love.

 Contemporary fairy tales—where anything is possible and where dreams come true.

Heart-stopping, suspenseful adventures that combine the best of romance and mystery.

 Humorous and romantic stories that capture the lighter side of love.

Look us up on-line at: http://www.romance.net

HGENERIC

Presents Extravaganza

25 YEARS!

It's our birthday
and we're celebrating....

Twenty-five years of romance fiction
featuring men of the world and captivating women—
Seduction and passion guaranteed!

Not only are we promising you three months of terrific
books, authors and romance, but as an added **bonus**
with the retail purchase of two Presents® titles,
you can receive a special one-of-a-kind keepsake.
It's our gift to you!

Look in the back pages of any Harlequin Presents® title,
from May to July 1998, for more details.

Available wherever Harlequin books are sold.

HARLEQUIN®

COMING NEXT MONTH

#693 1-800-HERO JoAnn Ross
Hero for Hire

When Lucas Kincaid agreed to guard the *very* delectable body of
writer Grace Fairfield, he had no idea what lay in store. Someone
wanted the beautiful Grace dead, and the list of suspects was long.
But his biggest challenge was making the woman who wrote about
happy endings believe that Lucas could be the man for her.

#694 THE PRINCESS AND THE P.I. Donna Sterling

Billionaire heiress Claire Richmond had run away to sow some wild
oats, only to realize she wasn't equipped to deal with the "real"
world. Luckily, her cousin sent a detective after her. With strong and
sexy Tyce Walker by her side, Claire had no fear…which only proved
to Tyce what a complete innocent she was, and what a rat *he* was.

#695 SINGLE IN THE SADDLE Vicki Lewis Thompson
Mail Order Men

Daphne Proctor used *Texas Men* magazine to find a husband—and
it worked! She was already half in love with cowboy Stony Arnett just
through his letters. But nothing had prepared her for the
overwhelming chemistry that sizzled between them in person. It
seemed like fate. Until Daphne discovered Stony *hadn't* placed the
ad—and that he had no use for a wife….

#696 SUMMER HEAT Pamela Burford and Patricia Ryan

Sand and surf, romantic sunsets, a house on the beach…and a sexy
stranger to share it all with. What more could you ask from a
vacation? In *July*, uptight Quinn could have lived without mellow
Molly, who showered naked outside and stayed up all night…. In
August, Tom wished Sally wanted him for more than just a passionate
holiday fling, though if that's all he could have…. *Two steamy novels
from two hot authors, together in one very special summer read!*
